Influenced

A modern retelling of Jane Austen's *Persuasion*

Jennifer Goodman

DEDICATION

To the original version, *Persuasion*, which includes the most romantic love note ever written, in my opinion. Thank you, Jane Austen.

Chapter 1

"Your mother is rolling over in her grave," Jane said as she helped Anne pack.

Anne shook her head defensively, "Dad couldn't help the market, and he never really had the head for numbers that mom had. You can't blame him."

Jane Russell had been like a mother to the Elliott girls since their mother had died 11 years before. "I can't help but think if he had let *you* help him instead of Elizabeth, you would not be selling your beautiful home and moving into that rental."

They were in the master bedroom sitting area packing books and mementos that had belonged to Anne's mother. Anne's father had not touched this part of the bedroom in years. It was like her mother was still here. Sun still streamed in the room from the giant picture window that was east-facing and overlooked the backyard. The sun was almost overhead, so it would get cooler in this room pretty quickly.

"It's not going to be that bad, Jane," Anne

defended, "Don't be such a snob. We will be right down the street from Mary and Charlie and the boys."

"That is what is bad about it," Jane argued, "Mary will have you babysitting even more than you have before. She'll find more reasons to be too busy for her boys because you will be so conveniently close."

"I love being with my nephews!" Anne exclaimed.

"Mary shamelessly takes advantage of that love." Jane closed up a box and put some packing tape on it.

Both women grabbed boxes and carried them downstairs. Anne's dad, Walt, and older sister, Elizabeth, were sitting on the sofa in the living room drinking lemonade. Walt was a handsome man. He had a head full of wavy grey hair and prided himself in his appearance. He worked out at his club playing racquetball, and swimming laps every day; and never missed golf every Friday. Elizabeth was a bit vain as well, and spent more time on her appearance than on the family business, which was probably why the family real estate investment business was in the tank. Her long blonde hair framed her perfectly made-up, tan face.

Anne glanced into the home office and noticed that nothing had been packed. She closed her eyes slowly to gather some patience.

"Dad, have you gotten anything packed in the office?" Anne asked with forced cheerfulness as she set her boxes down in the hallway which was almost full of the boxes that she and Jane had been bringing down from the upstairs rooms. She looked over at her dad, who had closed his eyes and furrowed his brow.

"Anne, please," Elizabeth whined, "give Dad a break. He has a headache."

Anne turned her attention to her sister, "Eliza, have *you* packed anything since Jane and I went upstairs?"

"Well, no… I've been looking after Dad."

"And sitting on your bum drinking lemonade," Jane put her hands on her hips. "Come on. Anne and I have been working like dogs upstairs. The least you both could do is get started on that office. That is *your* office, both of you."

Walt Elliott sat up and put his head in his hands, "I know, I know. I'm trying to get up the nerve….and the strength."

Elizabeth made a big, dramatic show of getting up and ushering her dad into the office, "Come on, Dad, we aren't getting any help from *them*," she glared at Anne as she passed.

Anne stared back, unable to comprehend why Elizabeth was being particularly nasty.

Jane stepped toward Elizabeth, "We have been packing the entire…"

Anne put her arm out to stop Jane and whispered, "Don't. It's just her way. She is just upset about having to move and doesn't know how to handle it." At least she hoped that was so.

"You are giving her *way* too much credit," Jane argued after Walt and Elizabeth were out of earshot. "You have got to start standing up for yourself."

Anne nodded, "I know. I've tried. I have found

it's just easier not to argue."

Elizabeth suddenly poked her head out of the office door, "Oh, Anne, by the way, the real estate agent left some papers in the kitchen when she came by. You need to sign them, too."

Anne wrinkled her nose. She had been completely left out of the house-selling process even though her name was also on the deed. Her mother had insisted that all three girls be added on to the deed with their dad when she had been sick. That way, if something happened to any of them, there would be less paperwork (and less arguing). When Mary had married Charlie, she requested that her name be removed. Anne smiled to herself as she remembered what Mary had said, *Charlie is filthy rich. I don't need this house.*

Mary had escaped the house eight years before and married the richest boy in town. Charlie Musgrove's family owned the town bank and countless other businesses in the county. Charlie's dad and Walt were old school pals and Mr. Musgrove had taught Anne's father and mother all about investing in real estate. Anne's mom had had a knack for it, and Walt had just followed her lead as a partner for years. When she got sick, and then died, Walt couldn't keep up with what she had done. He had asked Elizabeth to help him, since she had gone to college for two years and taken some business and accounting classes. Elizabeth was a good actress and had led everyone to believe that things were okay. About three months ago she had announced to everyone at dinner that they were going to have to sell the house to pay debts, and that all but one of their properties had been foreclosed on. The only property they had left was small, but was thankfully paid off, so they could move into it rent free, and start over.

She and Jane went into the kitchen and found an envelope on the counter. Anne opened it and took out the purchase contract. She gasped at the amount of money the buyers were paying for the house. That cannot be right. The house was not worth this much money in this market. Maybe it was worth this much two years ago, but prices had dropped. They must have really wanted this particular house, or maybe it was because it had more land than any other house in the neighborhood. Whatever. Anne was no real estate expert.

Then she looked at the buyers' names, Benjamin and Sophia Croft. Sophia Croft. Why did that name ring a bell?

"Anne," Jane looked concerned, "Anne. Are you okay, you just turned white?"

She knew that name.

No. It couldn't be.

Anne clutched the contract and walked swiftly back to the office with Jane following her with a confused expression.

"Dad," Anne opened the office door, "Did you meet the buyers?"

"What, Anna-bella?" Walt looked up from a box on his desk.

"Did you meet Mr. and Mrs. Croft?" She shook the contract in the air, "The people buying our house?"

"Er...No."

"They bought it without seeing it first?"

Elizabeth spoke up, "I was here when they came through. Dad was golfing."

"Where was I?" Anne couldn't wrap her head around this. She was going to lose it. All the feelings were rushing back. Before Elizabeth could answer, Anne turned around and fled up the stairs, leaving Jane standing at the bottom of the stairs looking up at her.

Chapter 2

"What is the *matter*?" Jane opened Anne's bedroom door and walked in carefully.

Jane was curled up in her oversized corner chair looking out the window to the backyard. Her favorite spot. The best view in the house. She was hugging herself. Her insides were in knots. The purchase contract was on the floor next to the chair.

She looked over at Jane and then back out the window. She didn't know what to do. Should she keep quiet about it and just act like nothing was wrong? No. It was too late for that. She had just overreacted and now Jane wouldn't rest until she knew the reason. Calm down.

Jane sat on the bed and waited. She knew better than to be too pushy. Anne was too sensitive and would much rather hide inside herself than share. She had to be patient.

Anne looked at Jane again, and a tear crept out of one eye and slowly traced its way down her cheek. She wiped it away before it got all the way to her chin. She shook her head and blinked her eyes hard as if she was pushing the tears back in. She pointed at the contract on the floor and said, "The buyer is *his* sister," and looked back out the window.

Jane was confused. "Whose sister?" she asked without thinking first, but as she said the words she knew. She could only think of one person that would evoke such an emotional response from Anne.

"Oh."

Then Jane got up and squished next to Anne on the big chair and wrapped her arms around her like a mom would, and held Anne while she cried quietly.

"You obviously still have feelings for him," Jane whispered to her. "How long has it been?"

"It has been almost 10 years," Anne wiped her eyes with a tissue, "and I still think about him all the time."

"I've been afraid to ask."

"I should have said 'yes,'" Anne said after a long pause, still staring out the window.

"You were both way too young," Jane shook her head, "And neither of you had finished college. I couldn't support it."

"I know." Anne turned and looked at her friend. "You were doing what you thought was right. But if I hadn't listened to you, I would be Mrs. Frederick Wentworth II. Rick and I would probably have more kids than Mary, and we would be able to help Dad right now, instead of his sister, Sophia." She pointed at the contract again.

Feeling slightly, but not completely, regretful Jane got up and went to sit on the bed.

"You know he developed that video game that is all the rage right now," Anne said absently as she sat up a little straighter, "He has really done well for himself. Just like he said he would."

"Is he married?" Jane was shocked that Anne knew so much about him at this point.

"No, I don't think so."

"You aren't sure?"

Anne shook her head, "I read a magazine article about him two years ago. He was dating some socialite in the city, but when I looked at the picture of them in the article, I almost didn't recognize him. He looked... vacant. His eyes weren't smiling. His eyes always smiled for me."

"Maybe you'll see him again now that his sister will be living in this house," Jane was trying to help by sounding hopeful, "Had he ever visited here while you were dating?"

"No," Anne sighed, "He never came home with me, and you are the only one who even knows about him."

Jane looked surprised.

"And it is going to stay that way," Anne looked straight at Jane, "No one else will ever know about this, okay?"

Anne stood up and walked to her bathroom to wash the tears from her face. When she came back in the room, she picked up the contract and sat at her desk. She signed the contract with a slightly angry pen, and stood up again. "And to answer your first question, I don't expect to ever see him again. He hates me, and will do all he can to steer clear of me. I doubt he even knows that his sister is buying my house. He made it very clear that I broke his heart and that he didn't ever want to see me again."

Anne turned and left Jane sitting on the bed. Jane remained stunned. She had not heard Anne speak with that much conviction and emotion in a very long time. Jane realized right then that she had made a huge mistake in persuading Anne to refuse Rick's proposal.

Chapter 3

Anne turned the key in the door of their new residence. She had just come from her last walk through her old house, now Rick's sister's house, to make sure they hadn't left anything. The movers had finished moving all their furniture the day before and now it was time to begin the odious task of unpacking. She knew she would be doing it alone. Dad and Eliza would never lift a finger. It had always been that way. The only help she ever got was from Jane, and that was only when Jane wasn't busy with her own life.

Sure enough, Dad and Eliza were in the TV room watching a movie. There were boxes everywhere. They had even moved a few of them aside so that they could see the screen. Walt had paid the movers an extra $20 to set up the TV before they left.

"Eliza, can you help me unpack the kitchen, please?" Anne asked even though she already knew the answer.

"I wouldn't know where to put anything, Anna-bella," Elizabeth said sweetly without even looking away from the TV.

Anne hated when Elizabeth called her that. Her dad was the only one who she tolerated calling her that stupid name. And even then, lately, she couldn't stand it when he used it either. The only time they used that name was when they were being lazy and wanted her to do everything. It was starting to sound like Cinder-ella. Anna-bella. The servant girl. I need to start standing up for myself, she thought, but only for a fleeting moment. What I really need is to get completely out of here and on my own.

Jane had been encouraging her to take a chance and take the state boards for nursing so she could get a job as a nurse. She had been putting it off for the last few years. Her family didn't even know she was that close. She loved her family, but she really didn't think they loved her back. She just felt used. As soon as I finish unpacking...

***

The doorbell rang while she was knee deep in unpacking the kitchen. She looked over the counter at her father and sister who were still watching TV, to see if either of them would bother getting the door. The bell rang again and neither of them moved.

"I'm in here *working*," Anne called out, "The least either of you could do would be to *get the door.*"

"It won't be for either of us, Anna-bella," Walt answered.

Anne came from around the counter, threw a hand towel at her dad, and mumbled as she made her way to the front door, "Don't you move a muscle, let Cinderella get the door for you."

Before she could even get to the door, it flew open flooding the room with bright light from the afternoon sun, and two really small shapes ran into the house and right into her.

"AuntieAnne, AuntieAnne!!" Charlie Jr (CJ) and Wally smothered her with hugs and kisses as she crouched down to hug them back.

Anne thought to herself, well, Dad, you *were* right. These two cherubs definitely didn't come here to see *you*.

"Did you come here to help me take treasures out of boxes and find homes for them?" Anne smiled secretly and whispered to the boys.

Big wide eyes looked back at her, and little curly heads bobbed up and down.

"Can you watch them while I go to the store?" Anne's sister, Mary, was a back-lit silhouette in the doorframe.

Anne squinted up at the sunlit doorway to see the door close, and was just about to answer in the affirmative when she realized that Mary hadn't waited for an answer. She hadn't come in. She had just closed the door and left.

Typical Mary.

Chapter 4

"Okay pumpkins, let's get all these books out of the boxes and put them on these shelves, then AuntieAnne will make you a smoothie," Anne raised her hands for the boys to give her a high-five. "You are the bestest helpers on the planet."

"Can it please be a strawberry one?" CJ asked politely as he grabbed some books out of the box and put them on the family room shelves.

"Of course," Anne nodded, "Is there any other kind?"

The boys shook their heads vigorously.

She wasn't kidding. The boys, even though they were only seven and five years old, were the best helpers. They never complained and they did exactly what she wanted. They would do anything for their AuntieAnne. Mary always complained that she could never get them to behave, but they were always well behaved for Anne.

She knew it was because their mother didn't pay

much attention to them, and whenever Anne was with them, they got her full attention. No matter how much Anne tried to gently convey that fact to Mary, she didn't listen or care. Anne wasn't sure which. Mary was more concerned with shopping and decorating her house. She loved her boys, but it seemed that they got in the way of her life more often than not.

Walt and Elizabeth had left for the club hours ago, and Anne and the boys had gotten the entire kitchen put away and were almost done with the family room. Anne wanted to get the common areas done first, and then she would start on the bedrooms. She would leave Dad's and Elizabeth's rooms till last with a hope that they would do most of it themselves out of sheer necessity. She was crossing her fingers, anyway. She could hope.

As they were finishing with the books, Anne's phone buzzed with a text from Mary.

"Charlie is dropping pjs off so the boys can spend the night. Having dinner at the club tonight."

Anne rolled her eyes. Lucky for Mary I never have plans. She wondered what would happen if one day she told Mary that she couldn't babysit.

I need to get out of here. I'm 33 years old. I need to start my own life.

***

It was late and the boys were asleep in the spare room upstairs. Anne was finally sitting on the sofa, with her feet up, sipping on a lemonade when Walt and Elizabeth walked through the door.

"We met the most wonderful people at the club tonight," Walt said to Anne as he sat down in one of the chairs.

Elizabeth corrected him, "Dad, I had met them before, remember?"

"Oh yes, my dear," Walt acquiesced, "The couple that bought our house."

Anne's stomach immediately tensed and she felt sick, "They were at the club?"

"Yes," Walt smiled, "and Charlie invited them over for dinner tomorrow. They were just delightful."

"Here?" Anne felt even sicker.

"No, silly," Elizabeth looked down her nose at Anne, "at Mary's," and she sat in the other chair.

Oh, good, thought Anne, I don't have to be there. I'll be the babysitter, of course.

Walt and Elizabeth continued insipidly talking about their newfound friends and Anne quietly got up and left the room without either of them even noticing.

She continued sipping her lemonade in her favorite chair in her room. The room was not as big as her previous room, but she had managed to arrange the furniture so that she could still sit in her chair and gaze out the window.

Tomorrow I'll look at the testing schedule, and register for the state nursing boards, she resolved. Maybe I could be working in six months, and move out.

Chapter 5

"I'm sure I wasn't invited," Anne objected, "You were the ones at the club. I was expecting to stay home and babysit the boys."

"What is the matter with you?" Elizabeth whined, "They invited all of us. What am I supposed to say to them?" She paced back and forth in front of Anne waving her arms.

"Good grief, Eliza," Anne rolled her eyes, "why all the drama? You can just say I don't feel well, or that I am babysitting, or that I am working. Make something up."

Elizabeth stopped and put her hands on her hips and rolled her eyes. "No, Anne. I can't do that. They specifically asked to meet you. Which… I don't understand why…I mean…I can't figure that out. Maybe they saw your signature on those purchase contracts." She was mumbling now.

Anne was shocked, but kept her face emotionless. Her mind raced; did he talk about me to his sister? And if that was true, why would they be seeking me out? Curiosity? She couldn't imagine.

"Besides," Elizabeth continued, "Mary took the boys over to the Musgrove's for a sleepover already. You can't use that excuse. You'll just have to come. That's all there is to it. You will not embarrass our family." She strode out of the room defiantly.

Lovely.

Grand.

Crap.

Anne got up and looked at the clothes in her closet and tried to figure out if she was going to dress to impress, or just throw something on that was clean. She hadn't shopped for new clothes for herself in quite a while because she was painfully aware of the family finances. Elizabeth and her dad had no problem spending money like it was water, but Anne could not reconcile such frivolous irresponsibility. It was just wrong to spend money you didn't have. Consequently, her closet was sadly out of style.

She decided on dark blue jeans and a nice blue button down with small flowery pattern. It was her favorite. The blue would match her eyes, and compliment her auburn hair. She had a lot of blue clothes. Whatever works, right?

When she got downstairs when it was time to go, her father and sister looked her up and down like disapproving parents. They were more formally attired, though not too far off from Anne's choice. Elizabeth was wearing a flattering, form-fitting, solid fuchsia dress with cap sleeves to compliment her blonde hair, and high heels. Walt was wearing khakis, a white dress shirt, and a navy sport jacket.

"You aren't wearing a dress?" Walt looked disappointed, "Go back up and change."

Elizabeth intervened reluctantly, "Dad, we don't have time." She glared at Anne as if Anne was deliberately trying to sabotage her life, and then turned to leave. Walt turned his back as well, and Anne followed them out the front door.

It's like I'm the family disappointment, Anne thought to herself, and rolled her eyes again. The eye-roll technique was saving her sanity.

She couldn't eye-roll herself out of the knots in her stomach, however. She had to keep reminding herself that it was just his sister; not him. And her entire, socialite family will be there to occupy the bulk of the conversation, so she could just sit back and observe, and be polite, but invisible, like always. She tried to distract herself with the information she had found about the nursing exam. She had signed up for the exam that was scheduled for one month from now. She would need to spend the next few weeks reviewing and studying.

She followed behind her father and Elizabeth as they walked up the street to Mary's. Their home was exactly six houses away from her little sister's, but the size difference was significant. Mary's house was twice the size, and was at the end of the dead-end street and slightly uphill. It also had a considerable yard with a beautiful pool, a tennis court, and a little putting green. Charlie had built an elaborate treehouse for the boys in one of the oak trees in the side yard.

When Mary opened the front door for them and invited them in, Anne had a sudden feeling of dread, and felt an urge to turn and run back to her house. She had noticed an unfamiliar car in the circular driveway, so she surmised that the Crofts were already there. She could hear laughter in the living room as Mary stepped aside to let them in.

"Sophia is so funny," Mary gushed, "She was just telling us about their adventure with their movers." She looked at Anne and wrinkled her nose. She whispered in Anne's ear, "Really, Anne…jeans?" Mary was wearing cream linen slacks with a pale pink, silk, button down blouse, and a long silver pendant necklace in the shape of a heart. Her high heels clip-clapped on the tile floor in the entry.

Anne decided to answer with a sarcastic question and an innocent expression, "You don't think I look nice?" She knew it would throw Mary off. Mary wasn't known for her quick wit.

It worked.

"Oh…well…yes, of course you look nice," Mary leaned in for a quick sister-hug, and then bounced away into the other room. Anne got a sideways look from Elizabeth before she followed after Mary. Walt had entered first and was already in the other room greeting the Crofts.

Anne wondered how long she could remain in the entry without someone wondering after her. She noticed that Mary had changed the gigantic floral arrangement that adorned the glass table that sat in the middle of the entry hall. She wondered how much *that* cost. She wished the boys were here so she could just run up the circular stair case that arced up to her right. She decided to use the powder room on the left near the double front doors to stall and gather more courage.

As she stood looking in the mirror in the powder room trying to stall as long as possible, the doorbell rang. She wrinkled her brow at her reflection as she wracked her brain thinking of who would be at the door. Who else was invited? Was it a delivery?

Before Anne could move, she heard Mary's shoes on the tile, and Mary mumble, "Where is Anne?" as she approached the front door, Then Anne heard the door open and Mary say, "Well, hello! You must be Sophia's brother."

Anne froze as she heard him say, "Yes, hello there. You must be Mary. I'm Rick."

"It is SO nice to meet you," Mary gushed, "your sister has told us all about you."

They continued small talk that Anne no longer comprehended. She could only hear his voice. The voice she loved. The voice that still filled her dreams. She grabbed onto the sink so she wouldn't fall down, and stared into the mirror.

Their voices faded as they moved into the family room. Anne watched her eyes in the mirror as they filled with tears. This was an unacceptable situation. She needed to leave quietly. She couldn't face him. She couldn't..

Someone knocked softly on the powder room door.

Charlie's soft voice was right next to the door, "Anne. Are you okay?"

She tried to hide the emotion in her voice as she whispered back, "How did you know I was in here?"

Charlie chuckled softly, "Because I know you. I know you dislike these parties."

Anne opened the door after she wiped her tears away. She smiled at her brother-in-law. He was the only one who understood her, and he usually made these get-togethers bearable.

His gallant gesture and warm, understanding smile gave her a bit of courage and she took his arm, and a really deep breath, and they crossed the entryway into the family room.

Chapter 6

Anne tried not to look distressed, and wasn't
sure if it was working. She looked around the room
for Rick and the Crofts. Before she could spot Rick,
a pretty woman a few years older than Anne
stepped in front of her and smiled, "You must be
Anne," Sophia Croft extended her hand. "Now I've
met all the Elliott sisters. The evening is complete,"
She smiled and looked Anne in the eyes as they
shook hands with genuine kindness and an offer of
friendship. "My husband, Ben is talking with your
father," She indicated the tall, handsome man
standing with Anne's father over in the corner. He
was holding up his drink in her direction in
greeting. "And that is my brother, Rick, over there
with your sister."

Elizabeth had Rick's attention with conversation,
but Anne knew that Sophia had spoken loud enough
for Rick to have heard her. In spite of this, he didn't
give any indication or desire to pull his attention

away from Elizabeth to acknowledge the introduction. Sophia paused a moment to see if he would look over, but recovered quickly and politely continued talking, making some excuse that Elizabeth must be relating something very interesting. Sophia was about Anne's height and had light brown hair cut to her shoulders. She was wearing jeans—haha Elizabeth—and a white lace blouse.

Anne was immediately at ease with Sophia as she began asking Anne all sorts of questions about her former home. Sophia was positive that all the good about the house was entirely Anne's doing. She said all of this out of earshot of Elizabeth and Walt, who were now both in a conversation with Mary and Rick on the other side of the room. Charlie squeezed Anne's hand as he let go of her arm and crossed the room to join the others.

Anne caught Rick's eye once or twice, but his face was completely unreadable. He had no smiles for her. It was as though they had never met. She wasn't sure how to process this. Her heart beat wildly when she looked at him. He still had that effect on her. She still loved him, and she didn't think that feeling would ever go away no matter how much he ignored her. She knew the reason for his apparent indifference, and she understood. He was still as handsome as he was in college, with his curly blonde hair and brown eyes. He was wearing jeans—haha Elizabeth—and a red button down with the sleeves rolled up.

During dinner, the conversation centered around the club, and on Charlie's twin sisters who were arriving home from college. Anne remained silent unless someone asked her a direct question, to which she would reply with the least number of words possible. Were it not for Sophia and Charlie, she would have been completely ignored.

At one point Anne caught Rick looking at her, but as soon as she met his eyes, he looked away. He still hates me, she thought. By the time she finished her dinner, she had calmed her heart down enough to be able to take a breath without concentrating.

After the group had finished eating and when it was sufficiently polite, Anne excused herself and began clearing the table like the servant she was used to being. No one objected, although Sophia looked a bit uncomfortable and offered to help. Anne politely shook her head and smiled. She gathered all the dishes into the kitchen and began rinsing the dishes to put in the dishwasher. Anything to stay out of the dining room and away from Rick.

As she was rinsing, she sensed someone standing behind her and was afraid to turn, so she kept working.

"You look good, Anne," Rick said softly behind her so that no one in the other room could hear, and set his glass down on the counter next to her. There was no emotion in his words. Just a statement of fact; nothing more.

She froze and mumbled, "Thanks," without turning around.

She was about to return the compliment, but he walked back into the dining room before she could say   the   words.

Chapter 7

Walking home, Anne could not figure out why Rick had been there. No conversation she was privy to during the entire evening included an explanation of why she was invited to this dinner or why Rick was there, and she had not asked. Those questions would have just sparked other questions that she was unwilling to answer.

She was certain that Rick had not told his sister about their previous relationship. Sophia had given no hint that she knew of Anne before this evening. Anne had been watching for some sign…a look, a knowing smile…but nothing Sophia did or said indicated that she knew who Anne was in her brother's past life.

She had slipped out of the house through the back door after she had cleaned up Mary's kitchen. There wasn't really too terrible of a mess since Mary had ordered in from their favorite bistro. She was no cook.

Anne could finally breathe and relax. During the evening, she had become aware that she was holding her breath on more than one occasion, and had to remind herself to breathe. Her heartbeat had been a whole separate matter altogether. She had had to avoid looking at him or her heart would flutter uncontrollably and her face would burn. She couldn't be in the same room with him and be comfortable. It had been an intolerable evening.

She didn't think she would be able to sleep with all of the wonderings in her mind about Rick, so she dug into her closet for her favorite landscape puzzle and set up the little table in her room so she could listen to her music in her headphones and put the puzzle together. No one would bother her, and she could immerse herself in the idyllic Swiss village in the Alps. Hours later, when she could no longer focus on the puzzle pieces, she collapsed on her bed and fell asleep dreaming of gathering flowers on the slopes near Zermatt.

Chapter 8

Anne woke to the sound of knocking.

"Anne!" Someone was shouting, "Anne, you need to hurry. Anne, are you in there?"

It was Elizabeth.

Anne opened one eye to look at her phone. 8:15. Well, at least it wasn't six. Elizabeth was never up that early anyway. She could count on her sister to never be up before 7:30. Elizabeth was probably shocked that Anne wasn't awake already.

"Come in, Eliza," Anne yawned and sat up. She was wearing sweats from her puzzle adventure last night and had slept on top of her bedcovers.

"Anne, we are leaving in…" Elizabeth burst in the room fully dressed, with perfect hair and make-up, "Good gracious, did you sleep in…? Why are you wearing...?" She looked around the room at the puzzle table, the made-up bed…

"Is there a complete sentence in there?" Anne started laughing. She knew she looked a mess and was unprepared and unwilling to explain herself to Elizabeth of all people.

"Don't be rude," Elizabeth snapped, "It's becoming a bad habit. Where did you disappear to last night? I'm tired of apologizing for you."

"Apologizing?" Anne said tiredly, "Whatever for?"

"You completely disappeared last night without saying anything to anyone," Elizabeth ranted. "I was embarrassed that you were rude to our new friends. You didn't even thank Mary for dinner."

"Oh, please," Anne mumbled, "I did the dishes. That was my thanks. I didn't feel well and knew no one would mourn my absence." She didn't add that no one had spoken to her all evening. That fact held no interest for Elizabeth.

"Well, I am here to help you pack." Elizabeth announced with a flourish, "We have been invited to the Musgrove's lake house for the next two weeks."

"What?"

"Charlie said his parents wanted us all there to celebrate the twins' graduation."

"For two weeks?" Anne was feeling overwhelmed. More big parties full of people who will ignore her. Well, that wasn't entirely true. Charlie always made her feel welcome, and his father was funny. Mrs. Musgrove was a love, but, with Lila and Henzie home at last, her attentions would be placed squarely on her daughters, Anne smiled and thought, to their chagrin, poor girls. Mrs. Musgrove could be smothering.

Elizabeth put her hands on her hips, "We are

leaving in an hour. Be ready." and she flounced out of the room and closed the door.

I though you said you were helping me pack? Anne thought as she heard Elizabeth close the door to her own room. When pigs fly.

She wondered if she could reason with her father and just stay home, but no excuse was coming to mind that was worthy of missing a celebration of the daughters of his dearest friends. She would just have to endure it. Maybe she could bring her nursing books and hide away in some nook of the giant lake house and just study for two weeks.

She began throwing clothes into a case. Actually, the more she thought about it, the lake house might be a nice break from being trapped in this house with her father and sister. It would be one thing if they were a close family, but since her mom died, they had drifted apart. Elizabeth and Mary were like their dad: social personalities, life-of-the-party, the-in-crowd, and lazy. And Anne was like her mom: smart, responsible, hard-working, and dependable. She wondered if they all saw it, and that was why she was so used. They all missed their mom so much. Mom had been the glue. Anne could never be her, and she was tired of trying to be. It was like her sisters expected Anne to be the mom since her personality was so like her.

Lake house. That was an understatement. It was more like a small hotel. They would spend vacations there as children. Anne got lost once when she was about eight years old in the basement playing hide-and-seek. That was when she discovered the indoor shooting range. She was hiding behind a big TV in one of the many rooms, and heard a loud pop through the wall near her head. It had scared her so much that she had come out of her hiding place and run right into Charlie, who was "it," and got tagged. Charlie, who was also eight, calmed her down and explained about the shooting room in hushed tones with wide eyes. He also swore her to secrecy. He had shown her the door that she was never to enter, and she had been afraid of that door for years, until when they were in high school and she had faced her fear. She watched the door one night for hours, and when she was sure no one was in there, she had opened the door to find a long room that looked similar to those shooting practice scenes in the police shows where the police have those headphones and safety glasses on and shoot at the target papers. She was in awe. There were rifles locked in a heavy glass case close to the door, and those same safety glasses and headphones from the police shows hung on hooks next to the rifle case. The target papers, however, were not silhouettes of people, but of deer at different angles. She was not afraid of the room after that.

There were multiple levels, and wings with suites of rooms for families and other single rooms with their own bathrooms. There was a giant movie room with real movie style seats, an indoor sports court with a volleyball net and basketball hoops, and an indoor pool. All of these things were also outside, but since the house was on a mountain lake near a ski resort, you needed to be able to swim and shoot hoops even in the winter, right? Well, maybe most people didn't need to, but the Musgroves did.

The lake was their backyard. They had two boats in their boathouse, along with jet skis and other water toys. Riding in the boats and on the jet skis was Anne's favorite thing about the lake house. She could sit on the boat and ride for hours. She didn't need to be pulled behind it on any of the contraptions available to those thrill seekers riding in the boat with her. No, she was content to just sit and enjoy the ride. When she rode a jet ski, she liked to drive because then she could control what was happening. She got thrown off once, when Charlie had turned sharply when they were going too fast. She was 14 years old. It had taken her the whole rest of the day to get the water out of her ears.

Charlie had been cavalier about it at first. What 14-year-old boy wouldn't? But later, after she had stayed in her room till dinner, he came to her room and apologized very sweetly, and made a big show of escorting her to dinner. They had always been good pals, but from that evening on, she noticed that he was particularly careful of her feelings. All through high school he had protected her and was really her best friend. She never felt romantic feelings for him. He was like her brother, and she told him as much many times. Elizabeth would always tease her, "You will be a Musgrove one day," because she could see that he loved Anne. And even though she would have been happy as his wife, she met Rick, and discovered what it felt like to be *in* love.

When Anne refused Rick's proposal and returned home after graduation, Charlie had resumed his attentions towards her. He was never pushy or annoying. He was ever so sweet and patient, but Anne knew she didn't feel the same way he did, so when he got down on one knee one evening, she had to tell him. He took it well, but was distant for a while until Mary came home from college and pursued him aggressively. She had always been jealous of Anne, and the attention that Charlie paid her. Mary had loved him for years. When he was sufficiently over Anne, he let Mary in, and they were happy together. Mary wore the Musgrove name well.

"Anne, we are leaving!!" Elizabeth yelled from downstairs by the door.

Anne opened her door and yelled back, "Five minutes please, Eliza, I have to grab my toiletries." Had it already been an hour? Anne seriously doubted it. Elizabeth was never one to look at a clock.

"Hurry up!"

The three-hour drive to the lake was quiet. Anne sat in the back seat and listened to music in her headphones. Neither Elizabeth nor her father spoke more than one sentence to her the whole way.

Chapter 9

"Anne!!" Henzie yelled as she emerged from the house and bounded toward the car. Lila was right behind her waving her hands in the air. The Musgrove twins. Charlie's little sisters. Anne was their babysitter when she was a teenager, and they were like her little sisters. They both looked so grown up. They were identical, but had vowed in high school to try not to look alike, ever. They wanted to be individuals. Their hair was naturally blonde, but Henzie liked to add low lights to make her a little less blonde, and her hair was cut shoulder length in an angular bob. Lila kept her hair blonde and it was long; almost all the way to her waist.

It was interesting to Anne how much she was loved and appreciated by the whole of the Musgrove family, and ignored by her own.

Elizabeth got out of the car first and barely acknowledged the twins as they ran toward Anne's side of the car. Walt was busy putting his sunglasses in their case and taking off his seatbelt, and did not even look up at the twins.

Lila passed Henzie and tore open the car door and almost jumped on Anne's lap. Anne could not help but laugh and smile at the sisters' exuberance, especially considering the almost complete lack of human interaction she had experienced for the past three hours.

She managed to wriggle out of the car and wrap her arms around the two girls as they began jumping up and down in a giant bouncing group hug.

"We are so glad you came," Lila said excitedly, as they all separated from their hug

"Daddy said that you might not," Henzie added with a pouty face, but her smile was back as she kissed Anne's cheek, "but we are so very glad you did."

Anne could not help but feel happy to be there, and be the source of gladness for her favorite girls. Just seeing them made her change her mind about coming in the first place.

"How was your last semester?" Anne asked with eyes full of love and interest.

Both girls started talking at once and Anne was barely able to follow two narratives at once, but gathered that each had successfully received good enough grades to graduate and move on with their lives. Henzie was really serious about a boy she dated her last two years of high school, and since they were still serious after being semi-separated while she attended college, it looked like a wedding was on the horizon. She majored in finance and her beau, Chas Hayter, was already an accountant in a big firm in L.A.

Lila had majored in dance and was on the cheer squad at the university for the last 2 years. She could do anything athletic. It made Anne jealous and proud at the same time.

With a sister on each arm, Anne walked into the lake house and straight into Mrs. Musgrove.

"My stars, if it isn't my favorite Elliott," June Musgrove wrapped her arms around Anne in a big mama hug. June was a big woman and her hugs were like being engulfed in pillows… jiggly pillows, since she was always laughing. "And don't tell your sisters that I said that." She pulled away and looked Anne in the eye and winked.

She said this same thing each time she greeted Anne and it was just understood that she said the same thing to Mary and Elizabeth. Although Anne guessed that because of her sisters' behavior most of the time, June really meant it with Anne.

"Well, my dears," June said with hand in the air, "we will have a full house for two weeks."

"Nonsense," Anne argued playfully, "This *hotel* could house a small army."

"A large army, too," Lila added with her arms outstretched to illustrate her point.

"And we are only three added to your eight," Anne offered.

"Oh my, didn't your father tell you?" June shook her head and looked at Anne sadly, "that man should be hoodwinked for treating you like he does."

Anne was confused, and wrinkled her brow. Who else could be invited? The Hayters? They were Chas's family, Henzie's beau.

"Mary invited her new friends: Sophie-something, her husband and brother," Henzie offered.

"And the brother is *hot*," Lila's eyes were wide and she was fanning her face with her hand. She pretended to swoon and Henzie laughed and caught her dramatically.

"So hot!" Henzie agreed as she brought her sister upright.

Anne tried to act naturally, but felt like she had been hit by a train. Two weeks with Rick in the same house, doing the same things? She was having difficulty breathing. The calm and peaceful happiness she had been feeling since she had been embraced by the twins was gone. Anxiety and fear had overcome her.

"My dear Henzie, her name is Sophia, not Sophie," June Musgrove wrapped her arm around Anne and started guiding her toward the stairs. "And her husband is Ben, and her brother is Rich...no Rick."

Anne nodded. She couldn't find her voice. She looked back at the car door, willing it to come alive and grab her and put her back in the car so she could get away.

"Jackson is putting your bags in your usual room, honeybun," June said as she got to the foot of the stairs, "Go get yourself settled. Lunch will be in the kitchen in 30 minutes."

Anne made her way up the stairs and navigated

the hallways to the room she always used. She and Mary would always room together when they were young, but since Mary had one whole wing now with her little family, Anne had her own room. It had a big queen bed with a down comforter and a high padded headboard. The room was big enough for a large window next to the bed and two overstuffed chairs. She had a private bathroom with a big bathtub/shower that was so big that no doors or curtains were needed to keep the shower water from getting on the floor. In the winter, the tile floors were heated for extra comfort. The Musgroves spared no expense.

She wondered where Rick would be sleeping, and if he had arrived yet.

As if in answer to her question, she heard Elizabeth's voice in the hall, "Why hello, Sophia. It is good to see you made it safely. Are you guys in this wing with us?"

Anne went to the door quickly so she could hear better, and held her breath.

"No," Sophia answered, "Ben and I are in a room on the other side of the house,"

Anne breathed out slowly in relief until she heard Sophia continue.

"I was just bringing this to Rick."

Oh no.

"His room is right here, I think."

Elizabeth then said, "Oh, his room is right across from Anne's room."

Anne heard her knock on the door right across from hers. The door opened and she heard Rick's voice as he acknowledged his sister and her sister in the hallway.

Anne slumped down on the floor right where she had been standing next to the door and put her head in her hands. Had June Musgrove known what anguish this room arrangement was going to be for her favorite Elliott, she would have never put him right there. Right there.

She could still hear his wonderful voice talking to the women in the hallway. They were discussing what to do after lunch. Well, at least this information will be helpful for the planning of *her* afternoon. I'll just do whatever they *aren't* doing. She tried to get a handle on her breathing to quell the anxiety.

It sounded like they were undecided, but leaning toward something lake-related. She would have to contract a sudden headache after lunch so she could stay in her room and study like she had planned. She began unpacking her suitcase and settling things in her bathroom.

After finishing that, she had about 10 minutes to spare before lunch, so she scooted her chair over nearer to the window so she could sit and look out. Her view was of the lake, thankfully. She never appreciated it when she was younger. There were two tall evergreens in the way, but for the most part, the crystal blue water winked up at her and assured her that everything would be okay.

Chapter 10

"AuntieAnne, AuntieAnne, where are you?" CJ and Wally banged on her door, jolting her out of a reverie as she gazed at the lake.

She jumped up and flung open the door to her two nephews and they knocked her down with hugs and kisses. As she wrestled and laughed with the boys she heard another door close and she became aware of someone else in the hallway standing at her door looking in, but before she could look up and focus on who it was, the person was gone.

"Come on, AuntieAnne, let's go downstairs and have some mac and cheese," CJ said.

Wally grabbed her head with both of his little hands for a secret and whispered in her ear—well, it was considered a whisper to him—"Gammy said we could have cookies if we ate all our mac and cheese."

"Goodie goodie," She stood up as Wally jumped on her back for a piggyback ride.

"My turn next for piggyback," CJ announced as he grabbed her hand and they made their way down the stairs and into the kitchen.

Everyone was already there, and most were already eating.

The kitchen had a huge granite island where all the food was laid out, and a monstrous dark plank wood table that could seat 20 if they squished. Mr. Musgrove was swing dancing--or attempting to-- with Mrs. Musgrove to big-band music that was playing in the adjoining great room.

Mr. Landry Musgrove was a tall, thin, happy man, who loved his wife and his family and would do anything for them. He worked hard, and played hard, as evidenced by the sprawling lake house and toys in his possession. When he saw Anne, he dipped June and kissed her, and then came to Anne with a deep bow and then a big hug, after Wally jumped down and ran for the food.

"So good of you to finally arrive, Anne-dear. The boys have been asking about you every 4 minutes since we arrived earlier. Wally even sat out by the mailbox for a while till his mom made him come back in."

"Good grief," Anne laughed and was aware of more than one set of eyes watching her. "Well, I'm glad to be the object of such admiration."

Anne helped the boys with their plates and choices and settled them at the end of the table away from the adults. She then collected lunch for herself and sat next to the boys and busied herself with eating and conversation with her nephews. She had no reason to speak to anyone at the other end of the table. The adult conversation was lively with planning activities for the next two weeks.

She noticed that Lila and Henzie had seated themselves as close to Rick as they possible could. He was, after all, a *hot* guy. Anne smiled to herself about that one. Rick would never have classified himself as "hot." There was no question that he was, but he didn't think so. She used to play with his curly blond hair when it got too long and hung into his eyes. She was always disappointed when he cut his hair. It was soft and curly and irresistible when it was longer and hung in his eyes.

"But we *must* wakeboard today. It is the *perfect* weather, and the lake is like *glass*." Lila announced louder than the rest of the conversation. She had her hand on Rick's arm and was looking right at him and smiling her best, most attractive smile, as if she practiced smiling in the mirror.

Rick was smiling back at her. Of course he was. No one could resist Lila. She was a doll. Anne wanted to believe that he was just being nice to Lila, but who knew? Maybe he liked her. She felt a twinge of jealousy.

Charlie spoke up, "Okay folks, let's go out on the boats and get some fun on." He winked at Anne. That was something they always said as teenagers. Let's get some fun on.

Mary rolled her eyes, "Oh Charlie, you can stop saying that now, we are adults."

"But, darling, we need to teach the good stuff to the next generation," Charlie answered in a laughing voice.

"Let's get it on!" Wally yelled in his 5-year-old

voice with his little fist in the air and everyone at the table either laughed or looked embarrassed. You can guess who did what.

"No, pumpkin," Anne giggled and leaned down to Wally's ear and half whispered, "Let's get some *fun* on."

"Oh," he looked at Anne and corrected himself, "Get some FUN on!"

The Musgroves, Crofts, Rick, and Anne threw their hands up and said, "Yeah," in some form or another to support the five-year-old. Walt, Elizabeth and Mary did nothing but look annoyed and embarrassed, but Anne hoped no one noticed.

Since riding in the boat was Anne's favorite thing to do, she didn't really want to feign a headache, so she figured she could probably finagle herself into the boat that Rick wasn't in. And the more she thought about it, the more she resolved to have a good time regardless. Why should his presence dictate her mood or her ability to enjoy the next two weeks? She was at ease with the Musgrove family and felt loved when she was with them. She was going to use that good feeling to help distract her from the fact that Rick was there.

She jumped up and grabbed Wally's hand, "Come on, pumpkins, I'll help you get your suits on!"

Both boys scrambled out of their chairs and raced their AuntieAnne up to their rooms so they could get ready.

As she left the kitchen, she could feel Rick watching her.

Chapter 11

"I still need to get some sunscreen on you, so don't get in a boat until I do, CJ," Anne held on to CJ's arm so he wouldn't run off.

They were making their way down the stairs to the boathouse. Anne had chosen to wear shorts and a tank top over her suit, since she was not planning on getting wet. She had an Angels baseball cap on to protect her face from the sun. Wally had run ahead, already lathered liberally with spf50.

"I won't," CJ looked up at her. "Remember last year when I got super burned?"

Anne nodded.

"I'm not stupid anymore. I'm seven. I'm getting the sunscreen this time."

"You were never stupid, smart guy."

When Anne and CJ entered the boathouse, she noticed only one boat, and Charlie, Lila, and Rick were sitting in it. Lila had on a cute red bikini and her hair was in one pony on top of her head. She had huge white sunglasses on that were silly, but seemed to work for her. She looked gorgeous. Charlie was helping Wally on with his life vest.

You have *got* to be kidding me, Anne thought. She took deep breaths to keep her heart calm while she sat on the bench and put sunscreen on CJ, and then when she was able to calm her heart beat down to only twice as fast as normal, she helped CJ get in the boat so his dad could help him with his life vest.

As she stepped onto the boat, it shifted in the water and her balance wavered. Charlie caught her, but she noticed Rick move toward her to catch her as well. She pretended she didn't notice. He's a gentleman. Of course he would try to help. Nothing special here.

As Charlie helped her find her footing, he said softly, "Sorry, Anne, your sisters didn't wait for you."

"Are you kidding?" she sighed, "that is not news and you know it. Don't apologize for them."

Lila heard her and added softly, "We are better off in the boat without the Elliotts."

Charlie and Lila both knew that the Elliotts were avoiding being in the same boat with the boys.

"Mary needed a breather." Charlie said with a knowing look and a nod, and Anne knew he meant from the boys, even though Anne had been the one helping them get ready. She even wondered what, if anything, Mary had done with her boys today.

"Is Henzie with them?" Anne asked. The other boat was bigger, but that was 7 adults. Anne couldn't imagine that she had chosen that lot.

"No," Lila answered, "She's talking to Chas. He

called just as we were heading down, and Mom didn't come, either. I think she is trying to listen in on Henzie's conversation with Chas…" Lila winked at Anne. They all knew that June had to know everything at all times.

"I hope she can get him to come," Charlie turned on the boat and Lila helped him untie the mooring ropes so they could get going, "He told her he was working on a big job, so he couldn't be with us."

"We can't wait for her?" Anne looked concerned.

"Who knows how long they will talk," Lila made that talking motion with her hands and rolled her eyes.

"Is Chas her boyfriend?" Rick said something finally.

Anne was not about to answer, but she didn't have to worry. Lila was already practically sitting on his lap. She would gladly use any excuse to flirt with him.

"They are practically engaged," Lila said primly and smiled glowingly at him. She started telling him the long version of the Chas and Henzie story.

The boat was making its way out into the open water so Anne went to the bow with the boys and sat with them so that the others could get ready for whatever apparatus was going to drag them behind the boat. She loved to just sit and ride with the wind and spray in her face. The water was glassy so there weren't many bumps unless they hit the wake of another boat.

Charlie tooled around the lake looking for the other boat, but gave up after a while. He had Lila drive so that he could ride in the tube with each of his boys to give them a turn, and then the rest of the afternoon, Rick and Lila took turns wake boarding and skiing. It was lucky for them that the others had gone in the other boat. There were more turns behind the boat for them.

She didn't want to appear as though she was staring at Rick when he was being pulled behind the boat, but it was necessary to watch for safety's sake, so she just enjoyed being able to watch him and not feel self-conscious. He was just so handsome. She could tell that he was still ripped even through the life vest. He was definitely still taking care of himself.

Charlie had trained his boys well, and they stayed safe and sitting, so Anne's job keeping an eye on them was easy. Wally even fell asleep after an hour. CJ was glued to his dad, watching him drive the boat so he could learn.

At one point when they had stopped to bring Lila in after one of her skiing runs, Anne heard Rick ask Charlie why she didn't take a turn. She assumed he didn't know she could hear him because she was at the back of the boat helping Lila climb on and gather the line.

"Anne?" Charlie answered Rick's question. "Anne doesn't ski or anything. She prefers just being in the boat. It's been like that since we were little."

"Oh." Rick said. He seemed satisfied with that answer because he didn't say anything else about it. Whenever Lila was in the water, Rick avoided speaking with Anne by sitting next to Charlie and talking to him, so that it wasn't obvious that he wasn't talking to Anne.

"Is everyone ready to go in?" Charlie asked. "It's been about three hours. Are we all hungry for a snack?"

CJ answered first, "Me, me, me! I'm ready for a big snack. Chips and dip and ice-cream."

"Maybe you can help me make cookies for desert tonight," Anne sat down next to CJ and put her arms around him.

He looked up at her and nodded furiously.

"Oh, Anne," Charlie added as he turned the boat to head for the boathouse, "we are all going to Marshals tonight for the big grad celebration for the twins."

"Yeah, silly," Lila gave Anne a high five and sat down across from Anne, extremely close to Rick, "You will be eating crème brulee tonight!"

Marshals Steak House. The Musgroves' favorite place to eat. It was the only place that would rise to the expectations of the other Elliotts. Normally the Musgrove family did not do highbrow kinds of things. Even though they were wealthy, they didn't act like it, or put on airs because of it. The Elliotts, on the other hand, with the exception of Anne and her late mother, acted like they were wealthy and tended to look down their noses at those who weren't fortunate enough to have the same bank account balance. Anne had to admit that the arrogance had gotten worse since her mother had died. Her mom was always able to keep her father in check, but Elizabeth had the opposite effect. Anne had hoped that their current financial situation would have humbled them a bit, but so far, she couldn't see a difference.

It was embarrassing, but the Musgroves seemed to overlook it because of the family friendship. Anne had often heard them say, "It's just the Elliott way," when they thought she couldn't hear. They were never too obvious about it, but Anne knew she was appreciated because she was not like her sisters and father.

As the boat neared the boathouse, Charlie slowed down to approach the dock, and Lila got up out of her seat to grab the mooring rope and prepare to jump onto the dock and secure the boat. CJ got up as well to help his aunt with the mooring rope, and Anne's gaze absently fell on Rick, who, she was surprised to realize, was looking at her intently. She couldn't read his expression and it made her uncomfortable. He looked away before she could react, so for something to do to feel less awkward, she got up to collect Wally, who was still asleep. He was small for his age so that made it a little easier to pick him up, but holding a sleeping 5-year-old on a rocking boat is no easy task. Climbing out of the boat with that sleeping boy was even more difficult than she had anticipated. Charlie was busy shutting everything down, so he didn't realize what Anne was attempting, or he would have stopped her. As she stepped up onto the edge of the boat and was in the middle of transferring her weight up, the boat pitched and rocked from the wake of a boat that had just passed by out on the water. She felt herself falling backwards and knew that she couldn't let go of Wally. She tried not to cry out and wake him up, but it was involuntary.

As she imagined what it was going to feel like when she hit the boat deck, strong arms surrounded her and held her up. For a split second she wondered how Charlie got over to her so quickly, but then realized it was Rick who held her.

"I've got you," Rick's deep voice was in her ear, and he moved forward to carefully propel her onto the boathouse dock.

Lila was reaching for her as well, and pulled Anne into her arms. "Goodness, Anne. That was close."

Wally was awake now, and wriggled out of the embrace he was sandwiched in. He hit the dock running to catch up to his brother who was already climbing the stairs to the house.

Rick kept his hand on her back for a few seconds to make sure she was steady, and then left them to help Charlie gather and carry all the towels and gear up to the house. Lila hugged Anne tightly, kissed her on the cheek and then skipped away to catch up with Rick.

Anne tried to catch her breath as she stood alone on the dock and watched them all walk away. She could still feel his arms around her and his breath near her ear. She sat down on the dock bench and put her head in her hands until the trembling stopped.

Chapter 12

Dinner at Marshals had been divine. Anne ordered her favorite filet mignon with sautéed mushrooms, twice baked potato, asparagus, and, of course, crème brulee. She kept to herself at one end of the table as far away from Rick as she could possibly get. She did not have the boys as buffers this time because they had stayed home with Jackson, the caretaker of the lake house. They were not old enough for Marshals, according to their mother. Anne had her father and Mr. Musgrove as dinner companions. It was all good. The men had talked to each other and let Anne alone. She rarely looked toward the other end of the table the whole time they were eating, and she had ridden to and from the restaurant with her father and Elizabeth. She did not have to interact at all with Rick or her sisters, which was just as well. The conversation at the other end of the table had been lively, and by placing herself where she did, she avoided being obviously left out like usual. Charlie nodded to her a few times and made her smile, but other than that, she enjoyed her delicious meal in peace and comfort.

Anne patted her tummy and smiled. Still feeling full of the delicious food, she was sitting alone in an Adirondack chair on the small balcony that was at the end of the hallway near her room. Her view was mostly lake, and some mountains. It was late, but the moon was close to full, so she could see the glittering lake and dark mountains and the millions of stars. She had always loved sitting on this balcony at night. Her mother had given her a book of the constellations when she was little and she could still find almost all of them in the sky at the lake house.

She was looking for Aquarius when she heard voices below her. Lila and Rick had been walking along the path under the balcony and stopped to sit on the bench directly under where Anne sat.

Anne could clearly hear everything they were saying and thought about getting up, but she didn't want to stop looking at the stars. She tried to ignore them, but then she heard her name.

"Anne used to babysit my sister and me all the time." Lila explained. "She was our favorite."

"She is really good with your nephews." Rick said.

"Yes, she is. And they adore her."

"She spends more time with them than their

mother does," Rick added, "From what I have observed, anyway."

Lila giggled, "Yes. Mary is not the mothering type. We all know that."

"It is good that they have Anne then." Rick added after a pause.

"*She* should have been their mother." Lila declared.

Silence.

At this point, Anne wished she could see their faces.

Lila continued, "Charlie always loved Anne. We all thought they would marry. They were best friends growing up. He asked her to marry him when she came home from college."

"What?" Rick's voice sounded strange. Emotional.

Anne became aware that she had been holding her breath. She exhaled slowly and tried not to make a sound. She was afraid to move.

"I *know*." Lila said incredulously.

"She turned him down?" Rick's voice was clearly surprised.

"Well, obviously, silly," Lila giggled again. "Charlie told us that she loved him, but didn't *love* love him. That was how he explained it to us anyway. I was always sad about that."

There was a pause and then Lila continued, "Don't get me wrong, Mary is a great sister, and she really loves my brother. And she is not as stuffy as Elizabeth. But Henz and I sometimes talk about what it would have been like to have Anne instead of Mary as a sister."

Lila paused. "Things were different when Mrs. Elliott was alive. She was a wonderful person. Anne is a lot like her mother. Mary and Elizabeth are more like their dad. We love them all like family, but we like Anne the best."

Anne could not believe that Lila was telling Rick all of this. She was torn between leaving and staying to hear more. But she didn't have to decide.

"Let's go get some hot chocolate," Rick said, abruptly, and they got up and walked toward the back door.

Anne exhaled again and took a deep breath and thought, *now he knows Charlie, an obviously perfect match, proposed to me and I declined. I wonder how he is going to take that information. He probably really thinks I am a cold, unfeeling human being.*

She remembered their last conversation.

They were on a balcony-like landing on one of the tallest buildings on campus that was usually only for faculty, but Rick had been assisting one of his favorite professors all year, and he had given Rick the key so that he could propose to Anne.

Anne had been dreading it. Her mother had been dead only 6 months and she was relying heavily on Jane for moral support and advice. Anne had let it slip that she and Rick were talking about marriage. Jane had grilled her about him and felt it her duty as a mother figure to discourage her from "jumping wildly" into marriage with a man she had only known for a year, and who didn't have a penny to his name. She wanted Anne to have secure future and owed it to her late friend to ensure that Anne did not make a mistake. Anne had been torn, and was ultimately persuaded to decline his offer of marriage, or at least put it off until he was more established.

"I love you with all of my heart," She had said as she held his face in her hands, "but I think we should wait until at least one of us has a job." She continued to explain all the reasons that made sense to her when Jane had rehearsed it to her the night before, but she could see that he had stopped listening.

He pulled her hands away from his face and turned away. He was silent.

When he turned back and finally spoke, there was a determination in his voice that she recognized from when he would talk about what he wanted to do with his life. He was so sure; so confident.

"I don't want to leave you while I do this internship this summer." His voice was soft and calm and pained. "I don't want us to be apart. This could turn into a great job opportunity for me. For us. In fact, I *will make* it happen."

He had taken both of her hands, searched her eyes intently, and waited for her to answer.

She knew he was right, but she also knew Jane was right. What was she supposed to do?

"I…" she stammered, "Jane…my mom… I miss my mom…"

She shook her head and the tears began to roll down her cheeks. "I can't…I will never love anyone else like I love you…but I can't right now."

Tears were rolling down her cheeks again as she relived that night, and their last embrace. She got up and walked back into the house and down the hall to her room. Even though it hurt, she still stood by her decision to say no. They had been too young, and in the back of her head, it bothered her that he refused to wait like she had suggested. He had been headstrong and selfish.

Chapter 13

The next two weeks went quickly. Anne kept mostly to herself studying, and Rick spent most of his time with Lila. There was a 10-year age difference between them, but that probably only concerned Anne, and she was not about to make her opinion known. She had a small hope that he would eventually notice Lila's immaturity, but he hadn't shown any signs of this as yet. She had started entertaining unpleasant thoughts of his soon being part of the Musgrove family. She knew she would have to distance herself from them if that happened. It hurt to think of losing a close relationship with the only family relations she had left. Even if they weren't her actual family, they always treated her as such, and she thought of them that way.

There were occasional situations where Anne and Rick found themselves together, and while it was a bit awkward, each seemed to be friendly and polite. They had even shared a laugh at CJ as he tried to wakeboard by himself. He was making the funniest faces, and Rick was trying to imitate the faces for Anne as they sat near the back of the boat ready to jump in the water if they needed to rescue CJ. It was nice to see him smile at her. Their eyes had locked for a second; until he looked away when CJ called out that he was tired. Anne knew she had blushed, and her heart had skipped a beat at that look in his eyes. She had to hug herself while Rick jumped in the water to help CJ collect the board, so she could calm her nerves.

Near the end of the two-week stay, there was a scare with Wally. He and CJ had been climbing the big trees close to the lake and Wally had fallen. It was after lunch and Anne had been in her room gazing out the window and finishing up the last of her final study guide for the nursing boards when she heard a scream, and then shouting.

By the time she got downstairs and out into the backyard, Charlie was carrying Wally up the hill toward the house. Wally was wailing and holding his left arm. All kinds of everyone were rushing toward them in a chaotic mass. CJ was crying and following close behind his father.

Charlie was yelling for his dad to pull the car around so they could get to the emergency room ASAP, and said something about Wally's arm. Mary was in a panic, and going from screams to hyperventilation.

Anne wasn't sure who to comfort. Her instinct was to see to Wally, but since Charlie had him, she thought she may be a better help calming Mary down. One wide-eyed, knowing look from Charlie confirmed her decision and she went to Mary and tried to calm her down.

"Mary, honey, it will be okay. It looks like he either broke his arm or clavicle," Anne spoke calmly and grabbed Mary by the shoulders, "You need to get it together so you don't scare Wally even more than he is already."

Mary looked at her in a half-daze and stopped yelling. She suddenly looked confused.

"What is a clavicle?"

Anne tapped Mary's collar bone.

"You mean collar bone?" Mary said condescendingly between breaths.

Anne nodded with a straight face. She wasn't going to argue with her. She wanted Mary to stop the hysterics. "Can you try to calm down, please? …for your son's sake?"

"Yes, of course, you are right." Mary nodded, but was still breathing too quickly. Anne made Mary concentrate and follow Anne's example of slowing down her breathing so that she could be calm.

"Are you going to go with them to the hospital?" Anne asked her sister. By this time the men were getting into the car which Mr. Musgrove had pulled around to the side of the house nearest to where they all were standing.

Mary closed her eyes and shook her head, "I don't like hospitals. You know that."

None of the Elliott sisters liked being in a hospital since they had watched their mother die in one.

Anne gently shook Mary so she would open her

eyes and then stared at her intently.

"No. …I can't bear it," Mary said as she stared at Anne in a trance. "You go."

Anne hesitated.

"Please Anne…"

Anne stared. She can't be serious. Wally was her baby, and she was refusing to…

She had no choice.

"Okay, Mary," Anne let go of her sister and made her way up to the car.

She swallowed her own fear and waved at Charlie to wait for her. The look on his face was telling, but she wasn't going to say anything. He had married Mary with his eyes open. He knew what he was getting into. He shouldn't be surprised.

Anne got into the back with Charlie and Wally and helped cradle the boy so the bumpy ride wouldn't be too painful. She began singing softly to Wally and running her fingers through his hair.

"Are you going to be okay?" Charlie asked her softly.

"Me?" Anne was caught off guard. Even though it was Charlie, she was still surprised that anyone cared about her feelings, especially with an injured 5-year-old in the car.

"Yes, you, Annie." Charlie turned his head so that she would see he was looking at her. "A hospital is not your favorite place."

"I'll be okay. I'm just concerned about this little pumpkin." She kissed Wally on the top of his head as he began to calm down a little, and the car pulled out onto the road. She continued her soothing song.

She was never aware of anyone else but Mary in

the backyard, so she never saw Rick, or noticed that he had been right there and had seen and heard everything. She also didn't see the look on his face as she marched up the hill and got in the car. If she had, she would have known that he recognized the pain and anguish she was going to feel when she entered that hospital, and that he was touched by her sacrifice for her sister.

Chapter 14

Anne was correct in her triage diagnosis. Wally had fractured his left forearm: the radius, to be exact. As they rode back to the house after being at the hospital for three hours, Wally was snuggled up to Anne in the back seat, asleep from the pain meds, with a bright red cast on his arm. Anne had held him while they set the arm. Charlie told all the hospital staff that Anne had graduated from nursing school, and Anne had been more than embarrassed to say the least.

"Thanks for telling everyone within earshot that I was a nursing student," Anne said to Charlie, who was now in the front seat with his father.

He turned with a sarcastic grin, "Well, *you* weren't going to say anything, you dork."

"Why is that even important?" She complained, "No one cares."

"I care," both Charlie and his dad said in unison, and then pointed at each other, "JINX."

Charlie and his dad burst out laughing. Anne smiled.

"Did you ever take the state exam?"

Anne stared at Charlie, and then replied, "No."

She turned her head to look out the window. She wasn't about to tell anyone that she was about to take that test. She was just going to take it, get a job, and leave. No one would care anyway. Well, maybe the Musgroves would care. She would keep in touch with them. They felt more like her family than her dad, Mary, and Elizabeth. She didn't think Elizabeth had said two words to her for a week, and they were staying in the same house, in the same wing. Sophia Croft was friendly and had sought her out for a conversation many times. She was fun to talk to, but Anne's own sisters didn't know what to say to her. She was not like them and they didn't know how to handle it. It was just as well. She didn't have anything to say to them either.

"Well, if you are uncomfortable in hospitals, maybe it's for the best." Charlie mused. "A nurse afraid of hospitals is not ideal."

"Not all nurses work in hospitals, you know." Anne countered.

"True."

Initially as they had walked into the hospital with Wally, the familiar smell and lighting had brought back the fear and sadness she experienced when her mother died, but because she was distracted with making Wally comfortable, those feelings did not linger and she was able to attach a different memory to the sights and sounds and smells of the building. She guessed that she would probably be alright working in a hospital after all. She had faced it and conquered it. She was stronger than she thought.

When they reached the lake house, Wally roused and bounded inside to show everyone his new "arm" and everyone was generous with their attention. Elizabeth even hugged him and signed his cast, to Anne's surprise.

"It's a hair-brain fraction!" Wally exclaimed proudly as he held out his cast for Rick to sign.

Rick burst out laughing and looked right at Anne, who tried not to laugh, but failed.

"Pumpkin, it's a hair-*line* frac*ture*," Anne whispered in Wally's ear.

Wally nodded confidently as Rick signed his cast, "That's what I said."

Anne was about to disappear upstairs and escape to her room when the adults began talking of going to Marshals again for dinner for the last time. Anne was starving. She had eaten a bag of chips and a candy bar at the hospital, but it was dinnertime and she felt it. Marshals would be a great end to a trying day.

As she started for the stairs so that she could freshen up and change clothes Mr. Musgrove was explaining to Mary what the doctor had said about bathing Wally with the cast on…

Mary interrupted him, "I'm not going to be here for his bath, we are going to Marshals for dinner. Jackson can do it."

"You cannot expect Jackson to do what the boy's own mother should be doing," June Musgrove said gently but firmly, "Wally's had a rough afternoon, Mary."

"What?!" Mary was incensed. "I am not missing dinner! I'm not missing our last time at Marshals because Wally decided to fall out of a tree."

Charlie stepped in, "Darling, calm down. You and I can call for them to deliver our dinner after we help Wally with his bath. It will be fun. Just you and me."

"NO." Mary was acting like a two-year-old, but this was not new to Anne. "I will not miss an evening with *our guests*. Anne can stay with Wally."

Charlie looked like he had been slapped and was about to escalate the argument when Anne called from the stairs where she had stopped. "I'll stay with Wally." She almost added, *because no one wants me there anyway*, but kept that to herself and just turned and walked up the stairs.

As she rounded the landing, she heard Charlie say, "I can't believe you, Mary. Anne is not our nanny. She is your sister, and you are treating her like a servant..."

Anne didn't hear any more. She trudged up the stairs and into her room. She was able to stave off the tears until she was sitting in her chair gazing out the window, and then she watched the lake glisten through blurry, tear-filled eyes.

After a little time went by, she heard footsteps outside her door and then someone knocked.

She got up and wiped her tears quickly and opened the door.

June Musgrove walked into the room and wrapped her arms around Anne.

It felt good to be held, and she let herself cry a little more.

"I'm sorry, my dear," June said sadly. "I know that you are never surprised by your sister's selfishness, but I admit that this time, I did not expect her to be this unfeeling. She wouldn't even go to the hospital with him. I am truly sorry."

"It is okay," Anne pulled away reluctantly, "You are right. I don't expect her to act any differently. Especially since I give in to her every time to avoid the confrontation. It is just as much my fault as it is hers. I let her treat me like this."

June nodded sadly, and added, "I am staying home with you and the boys. We can make a movie night of it."

"You do not have to do that," Anne objected, "I will be fine with the boys."

"Nonsense. I want to stay," June grabbed Anne's face and squeezed it, "I think of you as a daughter, you know." She winked. It was something she had always said to Anne even when Anne's mother had been alive.

"We will have our favorites delivered from Marshals and pick a good comedy to watch after the boys are in bed."

"You always know how to make things fun," Anne hugged June again. "Thank you."

Anne told her what she wanted to eat so she could get it ordered, and Anne washed her face and went to find the boys to get them ready for bed.

She ran smack into Rick as she rounded the corner to the wing where the boys' rooms were. He grabbed her arms so she wouldn't fall backwards.

"I'm so sorry," She stammered and stepped back away from him, "I was going to get the boys…"

"I was just coming from my sister's room."

Anne wanted to get away from him as quickly as she could, but he looked as if he wanted to say something so she paused and waited.

"I… We… Sophia, Ben, and I feel really bad that you are not coming to dinner."

Anne raised her eyebrows, "Really? I…well…that is very nice of you to say, but I will be fine, thank you."

"I know…" he hesitated but his eyes never left hers. "I can see now what you meant when you would describe your relationship with your sisters. I never understood before."

He had not referred to their past until now. She was confused, and wanted to run. Her heart was beating faster than she wanted it to.

She nodded and looked around awkwardly. He was still staring.

"My sister and I get along like best friends and so I just always thought you were exaggerating."

She looked up at him again and said very seriously, "We were both young and… immature."

He laughed, "And not very good listeners."

She wasn't sure what that meant, but she had to get away from him so she could breathe. She nodded absently, wished him a good evening, and walked quickly down the hall. When she turned and opened Wally's door, he was still standing in the hallway watching her.

Chapter 15

Wally wasn't in his room, but there was no way she was going to go back into the hallway and risk Rick still being there. She went to the window and looked out at the view. Wally's room overlooked the side yard. She could see the boathouse and a little of the lake to the left and the garage and the road to the right. It was a different view than what Anne had in her room. She sat down on the window seat and looked out at the different perspective for a few minutes. She thought about her encounter with Rick.

They would miss her at dinner? That was weird. She was always ignored in the big group. What would they miss? And what did he mean about being bad listeners? She was a good listener. Was he referring to himself? Because that was definitely true. He didn't listen to her explanation about why they should wait to get married. He had totally shut her out and focused only on his plan.

Regardless, he still gave her goosebumps. He was the most handsome man she knew, and had been her best friend. She hadn't had a friend like that since. Ten years. She missed him. He was right there, but she missed him. No one she had met since had made her feel that love that she felt for him. She would easily forgive him and take him back if he asked.

The door flung open and CJ was standing there.

"AuntieAnne! Come on! Gammy says we are having popcorn in the movie room!" He ran to her and grabbed her hand and practically dragged her in the direction of the movie room. Luckily Rick had vacated the hallway and it was only CJ and herself.

She spent the rest of the evening with June and the boys. They watched a movie about penguins on the big screen, and ate popcorn. The boys had their dinner and Anne helped them bathe and get ready for bed. Wally had some trouble with the bag she had wrapped his arm in during his bath, but it was such a new adventure for him, he didn't complain.

When she got back downstairs with June, their dinner had arrived and they sat in the formal dining room and ate their fancy dinner with the fine china and candlelight.

"See?" June announced. "We can have our fun without those stuffed shirts."

Anne laughed and lifted her glass to toast her favorite Musgrove.

After they ate, they sat in the great room and talked and listened to music. June was able to get Anne to talk about her nursing goals and Anne swore her to secrecy.

"Your secret is safe with me, honey. Believe me; you deserve to have your own life of happiness that does not involve being used and abused by your father and sisters."

"Thank you," Anne had found another person to talk to besides Jane. She was enjoying herself. She felt comfortable and loved.

But that did not last much longer. Within the hour, the rest of the group returned from Marshals. Anne and June gave each other eye-rolls as the others entered the room. Their peace was over.

The group was buzzing and excited about something. It took a minute to gather that they had been invited to the beach house of one of Rick's friends from work. One of his software developer friends had just purchased a house in Malibu right on the beach and wanted Rick to come stay for a week. The home was hotel-like, like the lake house, and Rick was told he could invite up to 6 other people.

Lila plopped herself down on the sofa right next to Anne and bounced as she said, "You are coming with us, you know. It is going to be so fun."

"Uh…" Anne tried to say something but she was having trouble. Lila was talking a mile a minute…something about her and Anne, and then Henzie and Chas, because Chas would be able to meet them in L.A. on their way to Malibu. And other people were going to be there. Guys. Anne couldn't get a word in edgewise.

"And my dad said we couldn't go unless you went with us. You know, like an old-fashioned chaperone, because he doesn't know any of these other guys even though Rick says they are good guys. I mean, like, one of them just lost his fiancé. She died in an accident or something. So sad. But we can all cheer him up. And Malibu, oh my gosh, I've never been there. And I am going to need to go bathing suit shopping…"

"LILA!" June interrupted her. "Can you stop chattering on for a minute so that someone rational can explain this?"

"Allow me," Rick said gallantly as he bowed slightly, grinning the whole time, "One of my good friends has done very well for himself in the software development arena and has purchased a large estate on the beach in Malibu. He has invited me to come see it and bring whomever I want for a week starting on Monday." He paused for effect and then added, "I would like to invite the twins, and Chas. And because Landry wants to be assured his girls are safe, he suggested Anne accompany us…" His voice trailed off as he caught the look on Anne's face.

Anne was trying to mask her real feelings, but was failing, apparently, because Lila suddenly said, "Anne? You don't want to go? But this would be so fun and such an adventure!"

Everyone was staring at Anne; especially Elizabeth, who would have died for this invitation. Elizabeth's expression was naked hatred, and this was all the encouragement Anne needed. Even though it would mean and extra week of watching Rick with Lila, the fact that it would put Elizabeth out, made her decision. As petty as it seemed, annoying Elizabeth sounded divine right then and trumped her discomfort around Rick.

Anne suddenly smiled sweetly and nodded, "I'm sorry, I was just confused. Of course. I will go. This sounds like a blast," and then looked right at Rick and said, "Thank you so much for the invitation. What a treat!"

As Lila threw her arms around Anne, Anne could see Rick's expression change to slightly confused. *He thought I was going to decline*, she thought to herself. How perfect.

"Well, what a thrill," June exclaimed as she stood up. "We will have to spend tomorrow at the store in town shopping for the three of you."

"That is not necessary," Anne argued.

"Nonsense," June winked, but her expression told Anne not to argue.

Everyone started talking at once. Henzie and Lila were jumping around the room in celebration and the Elliotts were smiling, but the smiles were forced. The Crofts and Charlie were laughing and adding their excitement for the younger people to go on an adventure. No one noticed that Elizabeth felt particularly slighted. She was the only single person in the room that wasn't going to Malibu, and no one had acknowledged it, but Anne was using it as a comfort. Mary looked annoyed as well, but couldn't really argue without looking even more spoiled and selfish than she had already demonstrated earlier that day. *At least she recognized that*, Anne thought.

"It's the least I can do after all of the hospitality you have shown us these last two weeks," Anne heard Rick say to June Musgrove amidst all the hoopla.

Henzie ran out of the room so she could call Chas, and Lila practically jumped into Rick's arms in a big hug that almost knocked him over. Sophia and Ben, sensitive to Elizabeth and Mary's expressions, began to talk about all the fun they were going to have when they got home. There was a tennis competition coming up at the club and Sophia asked Mary if she would like to be her doubles partner, while Ben invited Elizabeth and Walt to join him in the club's upcoming golf tournament.

Anne just sat there and tried to listen to all the conversations while coming to terms with another week with Rick, but not with Rick. How was she going to do this? She wondered what his friends were like and if she could find conversation with them, or would it just be another week of being ignored. At least it was at a beach. She could just sit on the beach and look at the water for a week.

She quietly got up off of the sofa and made her way out of the room and got all the way to the stairs when she became aware of someone behind her. She turned politely as she stepped on the first stair to find Rick smiling at her, "Thank you for agreeing to come with us," he tilted his head like he used to when he was happy. Her heart beat faster.

"No problem." She smiled back. She was eye-to-eye with him since she was standing on the step. "It will be fun to sit on the beach for a week."

"Jay says there is some good hiking with awesome views of the ocean and Channel Islands, too."

"Oh?" She said, a bit surprised. "Hiking is fun."

He nodded, but didn't turn away like she expected. He just studied her with an unreadable expression, and she was instantly uncomfortable. She looked away at the group behind him in the great room and then down at her hand on the railing.

"Uh…well, goodnight," She smiled and turned up the stairs. She didn't look back even when she turned at the landing, or she would have seen that he was still following her with his eyes.

Hiking, she thought, why did he make a point of saying that? That was something they had enjoyed doing together when they were at school. Like I'm going to be hiking with him…He is going to be with Lila.

She let the sadness overwhelm her when she got to her room as she lay on her bed and the tears quietly rolled down her cheeks.

Chapter 16

Chas was driving. Chas was a redhead, and a bit nerdy in a hipster kind of way. He wore thick rimmed glasses, and had intense blue eyes. He was rail thin and about 6'2." Henzie had not stopped smiling and staring at him since he got in the car.

Rick had driven from the lake house to Chas's place in Santa Monica, and Chas had offered to take over and drive the rest of the way. They were driving Henzie's white BMW.

The car raced past endless beach on the left. Anne had chosen the back seat on the left because she wanted this view. Henzie was in the front with Chas, of course, so Lila and Rick were in the backseat with Anne. Lila was in the middle but made a concerted effort to sit as close to Rick as possible so Anne had ample space. She had spent these last hours trying not to think about that.

"It looks like 2.6 more miles and then a left

turn," Rick leaned forward to tell Chas. He was
following his phone's GPS directions.

Anne looked ahead and could see homes
upcoming just left of the highway. They were on
tall cliffs above the beach. So, this place wasn't
exactly on the beach, but maybe had stairs leading
down to a private beach. Even better. She could
hide down there.

It was early evening and the beginning of a
sunset was already incredible. She could barely see
the Channel Islands ahead in the haze, but the haze
would make the sunset even prettier as the sun set
lower in the sky. The one good thing about smog…

"Are we getting dinner first, or going straight
there?" Henzie asked, "I'm starving."

"I'm tired of eating chips and crackers," Lila
added.

Rick looked at his phone for a minute then
declared that he had texted Jay and there was a
spread of Mexican food waiting for them at the
house.

Lila bounced up and down and clapped her
hands, "I'm dying for some chips and *salsa*."

"And guacamole!" Henzie added.

When they turned onto the lane where the beach
house was, there were big homes on either side with
little, well-kept paths on the beach side that led to
steps down to the sand. Anne couldn't see the water
anymore for the trees and buildings. What would it
be like to live like this?

Jay's house looked like a Mexican villa and was
not the smallest home on the street, but by no means
the largest. There was a circular drive with a giant

fountain in the center.

Three men stood outside the front door to welcome them.

All three were gorgeous.

Nice bonus.

Eye candy for the week.

Chas parked and Rick jumped out of the car and gave two of the guys a handshake and a hug, and shook hands with the third as he was introduced. Lila was right behind him and was being introduced as well. Anne, Chas, and Henzie had moved a little slower getting out of the car. Anne stretched a little as she walked over to the group.

"Anne," Rick casually put his hand on her shoulder as he gestured to the first guy, "This is my best friend Jay Harville, and this is Luke Benwick, and Luke's cousin, William Marks."

She shook Jay's hand. He seemed very friendly and someone Rick would be friends with. Luke was a little shy and looked a little sad upon closer inspection.

"Call me Will," William shook her hand enthusiastically and held on a little longer than he should have, and then added his other hand to the handshake when he said, "It is so nice to meet you."

The guys grabbed the luggage out of the car and the whole party entered the house. Lila never left Rick's side, and Chas and Henzie were practically joined at the hip themselves.

Jay took everyone on a quick tour and showed each guest where they would be sleeping. Each guest had their own room and bathroom. The girls were at the east end of the house on street level, and the guys were all on the second level down at the west end of the house where there were even more bedrooms.

The house was one story on street level, but extended two more levels down the cliff, and wrapped around the cliff face so that there were views all around. The windows were floor to ceiling in all the common rooms. The engineering was remarkable. Anne had to wonder how the house didn't slide off the cliff face. It made her a little nervous, to be honest.

There was old fashioned Spanish paver tile flooring in all the traffic areas, and incredibly comfortable, thick loop carpet in the family room and the bedrooms. The walls were painted to look like exterior stucco and the decor was a tasteful mix of beach landscapes and colorful Mexican art. The furniture was all oversized to match the large interior spaces. After they had seen the whole house, they all made their way back to the kitchen for the food.

Will had stayed close to Anne the entire tour. He was cute, and very attentive, making sure she understood where everything was. He had dark curly hair that was short around his ears but longer on top, and intense brown eyes. He was tall and athletic and had a short scruffy beard.

Jay was blonde like Rick, but was stockier, like a football player. The more she observed, though, the more she realized the stockiness was more muscle than build, because he moved like an athlete. He was also a talker, had a quick wit, and was often laughing. He had an engaging laugh. She found herself laughing along even when she hadn't heard the joke.

Luke had not stayed with them for the entire tour and was sitting in the kitchen by himself looking woeful when everyone came in for dinner.

He must be the one whose fiancé had died, Anne thought.

Almost as if Lila read Anne's mind she whispered, "Jay, is Luke okay?"

Jay answered quietly to only Lila and Anne, "He was engaged to my sister, and when she died suddenly last year he was devastated. He has not been able to recover."

"Oh, I am so sorry," Lila put her hand on his arm, "for you and for him."

"Thank you," Jay looked sad himself, "she died over a year ago, but it is still heartbreaking because it was such a shock. She was in a car accident. I invited him this week because he has been depressed. Cassie wouldn't want to see him like this."

Anne nodded in agreement, "We will do our part to help cheer him up."

Luke was just slightly taller than Anne, and had dark hair, but not as dark as his cousin's, and not as curly. He was clean shaven and had hazel eyes. Anne wondered how long the guys had been at the beach house because all three were very tan.

They all chowed down on the chips and salsa, homemade guacamole, chicken enchiladas, and beans and rice until they were all stuffed and laying around on the furniture like they had been in a sumo triathlon.

Anne was exhausted from the drive. It had taken them four hours to get from the lake house to Malibu. She sensed a color change in the room and opened one eye to see that all the windows were bright orange.

The sunset.

She gathered all her strength and got up and went to the big window to look out at the view. The sun was halfway set behind the land that was miles away to the west, but the water was sparkling dark blue and white, and the sky was every color orange that she could imagine. She pulled her phone out of her pocket and started taking pictures. Sunsets were her favorite things to photograph.

"Beautiful." Will was suddenly standing next to her.

"Oh yes," She agreed as she snapped more pics, "I love sunsets."

"Oh yeah, that too," Will was looking right at her.

She was startled for a second, turned bright red, and then recovered enough to nod and accept his obvious compliment. No one had complimented her for so long; she didn't know what to do with it. She even wondered how awful she must look after so long in the car. She felt stale, and bleary eyed.

But he thought she was beautiful.

Unless he just had game, and it was a line.

Anne decided to take the former.

"That is very nice of you to say," She smiled up at him.

"I only speak the truth."

"Speaking of truth, what is the beach like?" She

changed the subject.

Will tilted his head to one side as if to study her. "Now why would you ask that? Are you a surfer? A sunbather? An explorer? It all depends on what you want to do with it."

"Good grief," Anne started laughing. "Basic beach. Is there sand? Is the water rough or calm? Are there rocks? Can you wade in…? You know…spell it out for me."

"Did you just come here for the beach?"

Anne was now frustrated, "Are you going to continue to answer my questions with another question? I asked first, for crying out loud."

He grinned and stared at her.

She looked at him for a moment with an exasperated expression and then turned away and looked back at the sunset. It was fading and getting darker. Still gorgeous, just darker oranges. There were birds flying through it. She was done playing the question game, so she continued taking pictures to capture the birds in flight and hoped he would give up and leave. His attention was making her nervous now.

"There is a generous portion of sand and a small cove to the right of the house at the bottom of the steps. There are some rocks further to the right that create a tide pool of sorts when the tide is low. At low tide you can wade a little ways out, but at high tide it is pretty rough." He paused and then said, "We tried boogie boarding this morning and failed miserably. The waves weren't big enough."

Anne turned back to face him, "Thank you for that detailed report. That must have taken all your energy." She said sarcastically with a straight face.

He burst out laughing, "I like you. Cute and feisty. A perfect pairing."

She had to admit he was interesting and unpredictable, and a totally different exchange than what she was used to. It was hard to resist his good looks and charm, but there was something off that she couldn't put her finger on. She had to conclude that he was just a player and acted like this with all women. She was on her guard, but decided to enjoy the attention.

"I don't think I have ever been described as 'cute and feisty,' but I'll take it," she turned back to watch the last of the sunset.

He stood by her in silence until the sunset faded to darkness.

She said goodnight and he smiled and nodded to acknowledge that she was tired. She made her way to where her room was and glanced at the others who were all still passed out asleep on the chairs and sofas.

She was unaware that Rick had taken in her entire conversation with Will while he pretended to be asleep.

Chapter 17

Anne awoke as the light began seeping through the cracks in the curtains in her room. Her room looked out on the street side of the house. The twins had the beach view rooms on the other side of the hallway. It was fine with her to have a north facing view. She could see the mountain range and the sun didn't brighten the room as early and as directly. Her phone said it was 7 A.M. She had slept 10 hours.

She decided to get her suit on and find her way down to the beach after grabbing some fruit from the kitchen. She remembered there being a fruit bowl on the kitchen island.

There was no one alive at this hour. The house was completely silent, and it was just as well. She could explore and not worry about running into Rick.

She grabbed an apple, a pear, and a water bottle from the fridge, and descended one of the staircases to the second sublevel and then the third sublevel. Jay had shown them where the beach access was yesterday on the house tour. It was an iron and stone spiral staircase that ended on the sand. It was only about one more level down to the sand.

The sand was cool to her feet this early in the morning. The sun was up and shining a little above eyelevel. There was no haze and she could clearly see the Channel Islands across the water to her right. It was a beautiful, bright, sparkling morning.

Anne walked to the right and made her way around the cliff face to where Will had said the nice sand was. As she rounded the cliff, she saw she was not alone in the little cove. There was a towel on the sand, and a pair of flip flops. She looked out into the water and saw someone swimming about 30 feet out. The water was relatively calm and waves were not crashing, but more like rolling in.

She guessed the swimmer was male since there was only a towel and sandals. Women tend to bring a bag with snacks and sunscreen and a phone, and a chair and an umbrella, and…

Great.

Not alone.

Hope it isn't Rick.

After she had spread out her towel and sat down, she ate the pear and drank half the water. She had begun applying sunscreen when she noticed the swimmer was coming out of the water.

It was Rick.

Fab.

"Hey, Anne," Rick waved cheerfully, and shook his hair free of the excess seawater.

It was all Anne could do not to stare. She was thankful for sunglasses. He was bronzed and beautiful with no life jacket in the way this time. And dripping wet. She waved back.

He grabbed his towel and used it on his face and hair and then wrapped it around his waist and came and sat down *right next* to Anne.

"You are up early," Anne remarked. She was just a tad uncomfortable.

"I wanted to get a swim in before everyone woke up." He looked right at her and asked, "Did you sleep alright?

"Um…yes, as a matter of fact," She relaxed a little and laughed, "Actually, I don't think I moved all night. I was wiped out."

"Me too… all this traveling is exhausting."

And as if sitting this close to her wasn't making her crazy enough, he had the nerve to ask, "Do you want me to rub the sunscreen on your back for you?"

His offer caught her completely off guard and she didn't have an answer. Her mouth opened slightly but no sound came out. She just froze and held her breath.

Rick took the bottle from her before she had a chance to respond and began applying the lotion to her shoulders and her upper back. She was wearing a cornflower blue one-piece suit that had tiny ruffles that crisscrossed from the shoulder straps down the front, and had tiny white polka dots all over. June Musgrove had insisted on buying it for her because it was so flattering. The blue was almost the exact color of her eyes.

His touch on her skin was exquisite. She closed her eyes and tried not to enjoy it, but failed miserably. She missed him so much. This was cruel and unfair and she almost stopped him and let him have it, but she didn't. She didn't have the strength. Or the words. What could she possibly say that would make any sense? This whole situation was intolerable. He was acting like there was no elephant in the room.

He started talking about Jay and how his wife would be arriving the next day. She had been with her family at a reunion and had sent Jay and the boys ahead to get the house ready. Anne didn't think she even realized that Jay was married. Had Rick told them? Maybe he had told the others.

"You may remember her?" He added after his explanation of her whereabouts, "Sarah Smith?"

"NO!" Anne was surprised, "Sarah married your friend? She was in the dorm room next to mine freshman year, and a roommate sophomore year. Of course I remember her."

"I know."

Anne was shaking her head in disbelief. Tomorrow she would be reunited with a good friend she hadn't seen in ages. "Wow. You've got to be kidding me."

"I thought you might be happy about her being here," he glanced sideways at her, "something to look forward to, eh?"

"Definitely," She beamed as she looked out at the water, "I don't get much of that," she said without thinking.

Rick turned to her, "What?...What do you

mean?"

She collected herself and immediately changed the subject, "How did they meet?"

"Sarah is a writer for an online tech magazine, and she interviewed us two years ago about our software." He smiled. "I set them up."

"She remembered you?"

"Oh yeah," He screwed up his face in pain with the memory and brought one hand up to his forehead. "She let me have it for how you and I ended things."

Anne stared at him. Was he going to talk about this now? Finally?

"She was brutal." He shook his head and closed his eyes.

She smiled to herself and had to bite her lip to keep from laughing. Go Sarah.

Anne was thinking of something to say to keep him talking about it when they heard voices coming from the stone stairs. The twins. Rick opened his eyes and looked toward the voices.

Great timing.

"Does Sarah know I'm here?" She asked quickly.

"Yes." Rick stood up to go welcome the girls but looked down and said, "You will have a friend here soon enough. She told Jay she was excited to see you."

He walked a few steps and then turned back, "You should have a better time here than at the lake."

Anne stared after him as he walked around the cliff toward the stairs. He knew. He knew all along that she was uncomfortable and unhappy at the lake, and now she strongly suspected it was his idea for her to come here; especially now that she knew about Sarah. He had to have arranged this. He claimed it was Landry's idea for her to come, but she now wondered. *Could he possibly still care for me in some small way?* She mused.

She lay back on the towel and listened to the banter between the group descending the stairs and approaching her spot on the beach. It was more than the twins, in fact it sounded like the whole group. She even heard Luke's voice.

"Catch me!" Anne heard Lila squeal, and wondered what that was all about since she couldn't see the stairs from where she was laying.

As the group came into view, Henzie was shaking her finger at Lila who was being carried by Rick, "You cannot expect everyone to be able to catch you in those stupid cheerleading holds every time you say so."

"I'm learning," Rick was laughing as he put Lila down, but he looked a bit uncomfortable and wouldn't look in Anne's direction.

Everyone plopped themselves down all around Anne and either went wading in the water or slathered on sunscreen. Anne enjoyed listening to the conversations and answering questions when asked, but did not do a lot of talking.

Will had chosen to sit nearest to Anne; curiously in the exact place where Rick had been sitting. He was a willing conversationalist with the group and would ask Anne random questions now and then. Trivial stuff. Nothing deep or particularly personal.

It appeared to her that he was more interested in the group conversation and making sure he was a part of it, than getting to know her in any meaningful way. This was fine with her. He was handsome, and funny, but not her type. She still only saw Rick. There was only one Rick.

Rick and Lila spent most of their time over near the rocks and tide pools looking for sea life. Lila would climb on a larger rock and then fall backwards into his arms in a cheerleading style cradle catch. That had to get old for Rick, but she never stopped, and he was a good sport about it. He had to know that she was doing that so he would hold her for those few seconds before putting her on her feet.

So cheesy and immature of Lila to keep doing that, Anne thought. And so thoughtful and patient of Rick to endure it.

Anne got a little annoyed by it after a while and since by this time she was feeling like she had had enough sun, she started collecting her things to head back up to the house. Will was in the water when she started to leave. She didn't want to encourage him to attach himself to her so quickly, so leaving right then would be convenient.

Jay was playing Frisbee with Luke and noticed when she shook out her towel. Henzie and Chas were lying on their tummies and talking. Jay tossed Luke the Frisbee and ran over to join Anne as she made her way to the stairs.

"Hey, Luke, grab my towel when you come up," Jay said as he fell in step with Anne and they disappeared around the cliff face toward the stairs.

"Do you want to clean yourself up and then help me decide what to order for lunch?" He asked Anne.

"Of course," Anne smiled, "But I can make something if you have basics on hand."

"No way," Jay grabbed her towel so she could hold onto the railing as she climbed. "Guests don't cook at my house if I can help it."

Anne laughed. Best host ever.

"I hear you married my friend," Anne said as they entered the door to the house.

"OH YEAH," Jay remembered. "You already know Sarah… She is so excited that you will be here this week. She only knows Luke and Rick, so having you here will be fun for her."

"For me, too… Girl talk is always better with a good friend." Anne added knowingly. "She was my favorite roomie. I was sad when she transferred junior year."

They climbed up to the second level and Jay went to his room to clean up, while Anne continued up the other flight to her room. As she passed through the great room attached to the kitchen where they were the night before, she noticed one of the overstuffed chairs had been moved right in front of the floor-to-ceiling window. She only noticed because it was right where she had been standing the night before while admiring the sunset.

Odd.

That is exactly where she would move a chair so she could sit and look out the window like she did at home. Was this chair here this morning? She couldn't remember. No…she had used the other staircase this morning after grabbing her fruit. It may have been like this since last night.

Who had moved this chair? And why?

She was baffled.

Chapter 18

After showering, Anne donned one of the sundresses that June had bought for her last week: a blue fabric with all different size white and yellow daisies in a random pattern. She pulled her wet hair into a messy bun on top of her head and made her way out to the kitchen.

Jay wasn't there yet, so she sat down in the chair by the window with her legs underneath her. *I could sit here all day*, she thought. What a view. A vast vista of ocean and coastline. She couldn't see the beach right below the house because of the way the house was built into the cliff. It seemed as though the house floated over the water. A little disconcerting, but she got used to it.

She rested her head on the high arm of the chair and must have dozed off, because she awoke to a hand on her shoulder.

Jay was smiling down at her. He had showered and shaved and was wearing an Imagine Dragons concert t-shirt, and denim shorts.

"Looks like Rick was right about the chair,"

Anne raised her eyebrows, "I beg your pardon?"

"Rick asked me if he could move that chair last night after everyone had gone to bed. He mentioned you would enjoy it over here."

"How thoughtful of him," She was shocked, but played it cool, "I have this thing about looking out windows. He must have remembered."

She didn't have time to let this new information sink in because she had to help Jay decide what to order for lunch. It was getting close to noon, and she was suddenly hungry. They looked through his to-go order menus, and decided on pizza and salads. Jay placed the order just as they heard noises coming from below. The others were returning from the beach.

"Can you listen for the doorbell? I told Sarah I would call her around lunch," Jay asked.

"Of course," Anne replied, "Tell her 'Hello' for me."

Jay disappeared downstairs as Henzie and Lila came up and passed through the kitchen on their way to their rooms.

"Hi Anne," Henzie said, "Isn't this so awesome?"

Anne nodded, smiling. "This is a beautiful place."

Lila shared the plans for the rest of the day. "We are going to eat lunch and then go walk around the pier and look at the shops. Will says there are art galleries and a local artist street fair on the boardwalk."

"That sounds delightful," Anne said, and added that pizza was on its way.

"Fan-TAS-tic. I'm starving," Henzie exclaimed as they headed to their rooms.

Anne sat back in her chair and looked out at the ocean while she waited for the pizza.

After about 30 minutes the doorbell rang and Anne collected the pizza and salad, and was busy arranging it on the kitchen island when Jay, Will, and Luke entered the room.

"Perfect timing if I do say so myself," Will high-fived Luke and Jay and reached for a slice.

"Hold on," Anne stopped him, "Shouldn't we wait for everyone?"

He started to say something and stopped himself, and then agreed, "Of course, where are my manners."

Jay went to a panel on the wall near the light switches and pushed a button and said, "Pizza is HERE, people."

Anne heard his voice echo in other parts of the house.

Intercom.

Nice.

Old-school.

But, nice.

The others appeared within five minutes, which just proves that pizza has a strong gravitational pull.

Anne ate a piece of pizza while standing at the island next to the food, and then dished up some salad and took it over to "her" chair to eat it while looking out at the ocean.

Her reverie was interrupted after a few minutes.

"How did this chair get here?" Will was standing next to the chair. He half-sat on the arm of the chair that was opposite the arm she was leaning into, and took a bite of pizza.

"I don't really know," She lied, "but I like it." She wasn't about to explain the whole thing to Will.

He stayed there thoughtfully and finished his slice while looking out at the ocean. When he was done eating, he walked back to the kitchen, wiped his hands on a paper towel and then began dragging the matching chair over to where Anne was sitting so that the chairs were side by side.

Anne watched this with wide eyes. She was sure that Rick had asked Jay's permission before moving furniture. This guy just did what he wanted.

You could learn so much about a person without them saying a word.

"There should really be chairs here anyway, with this view," Will declared as he plopped down in his new chair, "Right?"

Anne just stared, but he didn't look at her for approval.

He started talking about himself, answering questions that she hadn't asked. She found that all she had to do was nod now and then while she gazed at the ocean. A small group of kayakers was about 50 feet out and paddling west, which was interesting to watch, and every now and then she saw dolphins out beyond the kayakers. Conversation with Will did not require participation.

She learned that he had been staying with Luke for the last few months. He was from Kansas, and had come to Hollywood to be an actor. He had been his high school basketball star, but had injured his Achilles tendon which took him off his college team, and therefore trashed his NBA dreams. He had enjoyed acting in a college drama production, and so decided when he graduated in general studies to impose on his cousin, Luke, who conveniently lived in Burbank. His looks had gotten him three commercials so far, for which he was very proud. His anticipated profession further explained his personality. He looked and talked like an actor.

Why he was talking to her, she couldn't imagine. His personality fit with Lila better than herself, but then he probably thought Lila was taken since she was attached to Rick at the hip. Great. She was stuck with him. Maybe when Sarah arrived tomorrow, she could shake him off.

"…and then they told me that I needed to cut my hair shorter on the sides for the next one." Will sat forward in his chair and looked right at Anne, "Do you want a drink?"

A response was finally required, "Sure. Water would be great. Thank you."

He nodded and jumped up. She watched him walk back to the kitchen so she had a reason to turn and see where everyone else was. Jay, Luke, Henzie and Chas were sitting at the big table. Henzie was waving her arms as she spoke animatedly about something and the men all appeared extremely interested in what she was saying. Rick and Lila sat at the island on the barstools. Their backs were to Anne, but they didn't look like they were talking to each other, just listening to Henzie, or looking out the window that faced the mountains.

When Will passed the island to get to the fridge, Rick turned and looked around and caught Anne's gaze. She smiled and nodded. He grinned and nodded back but didn't look away. She patted the chair and mouthed, "thank you."

He looked surprised for a minute, and then smiled differently. A content and peaceful smile. He got up and walked over to Anne and sat in the other chair.

"I'm glad you like it."

"You remembered."

"I try." He looked like he was going to say something else, but Will returned with the water and stood there like he was waiting for his chair back.

Before Rick had to give up the chair Jay said, "Hey guys, let's go down to the pier and walk around. Grab what you need and let's meet out in front in 15."

Will handed Anne her water with a nod and she thanked him. He headed toward the stairs with Luke and Chas to go get ready.

Anne and Rick got up and went back to the kitchen to help clean up the lunch mess.

Lila and Henzie had already disappeared so it was only Jay in the kitchen with them. They gathered up the trash and glasses and Anne wiped down the counter and table in silence. She started for her room and got halfway to the hallway when she thought to turn and thank Jay for lunch.

"Thank you, Anne," both men said in unison as she turned.

"JINKS!" Jay and Rick laughed and gave each other a high five.

Anne laughed and added, "Thank you for lunch, Jay, and for inviting us to your beautiful home."

"So glad you are all here," Jay graciously bowed, "we are going to have a fun week."

Anne smiled at both of them and as she turned to go, she caught Rick's expression. He was looking at her like he used to look at her. She only saw his face for a split second because she was turning, and was mad at herself for turning so quickly. She missed that look. What did that mean? She was confused now, more than ever.

She wondered how much Jay knew about her and Rick. She wondered if Sarah had told him. She had to have said something knowing that both she and Rick would be here together for a full week. But then, wouldn't Jay be acting differently? She had refused his friend's proposal. There was a loyalty there, right? Were guys protective of each other like girls were? It didn't make sense to her how they both were acting. In her heart she felt like Rick was warming up to her. His expressions...his smiles...his thoughtfulness...

She looked at herself in the mirror when she got to her room.

Eww.

No make-up...hair in disarray... "It is a wonder anyone is even speaking with you," she said to her reflection.

This was going to change.

She got out her make-up bag and touched up her face with some concealer and powder, added some eyeshadow, eyeliner, and mascara, and a little lip gloss after brushing her teeth.

With her face improved upon, her hair actually looked hip and deliberate, so she left it. Even so, Elizabeth would have a heart attack if she saw her in public looking like this.

A thought suddenly occurred to her. It was amazing how wonderful she felt out from under the oppression of her family. She wasn't worried about what her dad or sisters would say to her. She was free of the weight of criticism and judgement.

She was more determined than ever to pass the nursing boards.

Chapter 19

Will had characteristically insisted on taking her arm while they walked around the pier. Intolerable, but she refused to be rude. Rick appeared not to notice. He was ahead of them with Lila on his arm, anyway.

Lila was overly exuberant in her flirtations. Anne didn't remember her being this way growing up, but she had only seen Lila during summer vacations for the last few years when it was only family. She was getting on *Anne's* nerves and Anne loved her like a sister. Anne couldn't imagine how annoyed Rick was, but he was being a gentleman.

They walked the pier and stood on the end for quite a while enjoying the water and watching for dolphins. Sipping smoothies from the restaurant on the pier, they made their way back to the beach and decided to walk a bit on the sand.

There was a short staircase with a middle landing down to the sand and as Rick hit the end of the stairs, Lila called to him, "Catch me" and she jumped backwards into his arms from the landing. He almost didn't get turned around fast enough, and barely caught her. Anne saw him say something in Lulu's ear as he was setting her down, and she nodded seriously.

"Why does she keep doing that?" Will asked Anne as he fell in step with her on the sand. "It's a little annoying."

Anne kept her feelings to herself but explained, "Lila was a cheerleader in college. She and Henzie just graduated. I think she misses being tossed around."

"She was a flyer?" Will asked.

"You know the lingo?"

"My girlfriend in high school was a cheerleader," Will said, "but she was too tall to be one of the flyers. She was a spotter."

"Yes, I believe Lila was a flyer."

Will shook his head and rolled his eyes.

No patience.

"You have pretty eyes." Will said after a few steps.

"Thank you," Anne forced herself to say. He was smooth and charming, but she wasn't buying it. There was something about him that wasn't genuine. It was just a feeling, but she trusted her gut. Maybe he was just trying too hard, but maybe he was just trying to rush a connection for a weeklong fling. If that was true, he had chosen the wrong girl.

If he kept up the pursuit, she would have to say something, but for now she would continue to be polite.

They walked along the hard sand left over from the high tide, close to where the waves were breaking. It was easier to walk on hard sand with shoes. It was a lovely afternoon; not too hot, and there was a nice breeze coming off the water.

After walking on the sand to the end of the boardwalk of shops, they crossed the sand up to the boardwalk and started back toward the pier meandering through the shops and art festival vendors. The group gradually separated as some stopped to look at things, while others kept walking. Henzie and Chas disappeared altogether pretty quickly. Anne suspected the jewelry shop had something to do with it.

Jay and Luke stopped to talk to a long board vendor, and Lila pulled Rick into a bathing suit store. Really? Anne was embarrassed for him, but couldn't help but suppress a smile thinking of his discomfort.

Anne continued along the boardwalk and stopped now and then to look at art and trinket vendors while Will followed her like a little puppy. He tried to engage her in conversation, and she was polite, but didn't really give up anything meaningful. He didn't strike her as one looking for meaning, so she didn't feel bad.

She was examining a coral necklace that she was considering buying when he leaned toward her and said in her ear, "Anne, I like you. Would you consider…I mean … would you let me…can I hold your hand?"

She laughed out loud as she looked up from the

necklace, "What are you, the Beatles?" and then noticed the look on his face. He was serious.

"Oh, Will…I'm sorry I laughed, I thought you were making a joke." She put the necklace down and faced him in all seriousness. "Look, I have only known you a day, and you are asking to hold my hand. I think that you are sweet and handsome..." she grasped at the air for some nice adjectives, "and charming" …*and creepy and a player*…

"But…?"

"But I don't normally move that fast in a relationship, and I would be uncomfortable with what you are asking."

"Relationship…?" Will looked uncomfortable now. "I wasn't…not a relationship…I was just looking for... We are only going to be here a week."

"Exactly," she reached out and touched his arm, "And I think we should enjoy this week as friends and that is all."

He looked slightly bugged, but tried to hide it by nodding and agreeing.

"Friends then," he smiled and held out his arms for a hug that she reluctantly allowed.

What a jerk. She was correct. He was a player. What was the hug all about? It seemed to fly in the face of what she had just said. Thoughtless.

She went back to looking at the necklace and Will stayed with her, but started talking with the girl in the next booth.

She never knew that Rick had been about 30 yards away and had seen her laugh and then give Will a hug. She never saw the frustrated look on his face.

Influenced

Chapter 20

Now that she had an understanding with Will, things got less uncomfortable. He still remained attentive, but he was less creepy about it and actually more pleasant to be around. It was almost as if he thought she expected him to pursue her, and was relieved that she had stopped him. Weird. What was it about really handsome guys and their own expectations that they were supposed to always be with a girl?

They had dinner at the restaurant on the pier and discussed their plans for the next day. Jay suggested they hike a trail on the other side of PCH that would take them up where they could see the coastline from Santa Monica, the Channel Islands, and maybe even Santa Barbara.

Anne noticed during dinner that Rick was acting a little differently. The friendly easiness from earlier was gone. He wouldn't look her in the eye, and he wasn't talking; not even to Lila. Something had happened.

When they all got back to the house, Anne sat in her chair to watch the sunset. Will, Jay, and Luke went down to the second sublevel to play pool, and the twins and Chas were headed down to the movie room after they made some popcorn.

She assumed that Rick had joined the guys downstairs, or was going to watch the movie with Lila, when she heard Lila say to Chas, "Ricky has a headache, so he is going to lie down and see if he can shake it."

A headache?

That may explain his behavior at dinner.

Ricky?

She had to smile at "Ricky." He only allowed his mom to call him that. He was either being nice, or didn't know Lila was using that nickname.

When the popcorn popped and they went downstairs, she was finally alone with the sunset. She relaxed and was able to enjoy the view and think. What a day. She was feeling more comfortable with Rick, and she had quelled the Will situation. Sarah would be there sometime tomorrow. Her week was looking up.

She was playing with the camera settings on her phone when Rick came from behind and sat in the other chair.

Startled, she smiled and said, "Hello *Ricky*." She was unable to get that out without giggling, "Is your headache gone?"

"Ricky?" He looked at her, annoyed.

"Lila is calling you Ricky now."

He rolled his eyes, "Great….and, no, I didn't

have a headache, I just needed a minute to myself." He put his head in his hands and ran his fingers through his hair. "Look, don't tell Lila I said that. I don't want to hurt her feelings."

Anne shook her head, "Of course not."

He looked up at her for a second like he wanted to say something, and then looked away.

She watched him curiously and waited.

As he looked wistfully out at the sunset, he said, "I just came up here to say...to tell you... that I'm glad you have found a... friend here..." After a moment's pause, he looked her right in the eyes for at least a full minute without a word.

Her heart was racing. What the heck was he talking about?

"What are you talking about?" She had to ask. He was making no sense. "Sarah doesn't get here till tomorrow."

He looked a little confused, shook his head slightly, stood up, and walked to the stairs, stopped for a second, and then descended the stairs without turning back.

Anne stared after him. What just happened?

Chapter 21

Anne had trouble sleeping trying to decipher why Rick had acted so differently and said those things to her. What could possibly have happened between lunch and dinner? She could not come up with anything. She finally fell asleep and had dreams of cheerleaders climbing up into elaborate human pyramids and falling into never ending pits of darkness with no one to catch them, and then she was waiting at the bottom so she could catch them, but none ever appeared.

She was still trying to shake those dreams as she hiked up the trail. It was midday and had started getting hot. It was decidedly warmer on the mountain than down by the water. They all had ample water bottles in their packs, and Jay had offered to share a closet full of ball caps, so she wasn't worried about heat stroke. She wasn't used to this much exercise, and the rising heat made it harder to climb. At home she walked every so often, but not regularly enough to be considered in shape. She hated the club, so she never went, and even wondered if her father had renewed her membership.

The twins, Chas, Rick, and Luke were way ahead of her up the trail. Will and Jay had stayed behind with her and she was feeling stupid for even attempting this.

"Look, guys," She huffed during a stop at one of the switchbacks, "You go on ahead. I will be fine. I'll just stay right here until you all come back down."

Will laughed out loud, "Are you KIDDING?"

"We are not leaving you alone, Anne. Sarah would throw me in a pit of rabid rattlesnakes," Jay added with real fear in his voice.

"I just didn't realize that it would be this strenuous," She drank some water then added, "And it doesn't help that I appear more capable than I actually am."

"Nonsense," Will was being more gallant than expected. "This is a team effort. We are *all* getting to the top today. No fair maidens left behind."

"We can even carry you part of the way. Fireman style," Jay added.

"Not on your life or over my dead body!"

Both men laughed at that.

Will bent down so his face was even with hers and said softly, "Seriously, just go slow. We are in no hurry."

"I like going slow, anyway," Jay agreed in all seriousness. "This is not a competition."

"It is an adventure to be enjoyed," Will opened

his arms at the vista that was already before them. He was right. They were up high enough that she could already see the islands more clearly, and parts of the Santa Monica skyline were on the hazy eastern horizon.

"Quick selfie for Sarah," Jay gathered them together with the ocean behind them and held out his phone. After texting it to his wife, he put his phone away and took a swig of water.

It made Anne feel very special that these two guys were being such gentlemen and treating her like a China doll. She smiled as they started up the next switchback.

The three of them took it slow and steady and the guys distracted Anne with their extensive movie quote knowledge. Each would try to come up with a quote that the other one didn't know. It was rare for one of them to be stumped. Anne was surprised that she was able to identify most of the quotes as well.

"You're really weird," Jay said.

"Is that a quote? Or are you making a character statement?" Will laughed.

Anne interrupted, "Willy Wonka."

"HEY," both guys high-fived her.

"I have one, and you are not going to get it," Anne offered between steps. She was having to breathe for each step.

"Bring it on," Jay stepped out in front of her and walked backwards.

"You'll never be one of them."

Silence. Both guys were thinking. They all took about 15 steps.

She doubted either of them had seen the Sound

of Music enough times as boys to recognize the line, if they had even seen it at all. It was not fair, but she had to stump them with something. Most of their movies had been in the adventure, sci-fi, and horror categories. No chick flicks.

"Where have I heard that?"

"It sounds really familiar."

"It *does not*," She laughed at them. "You have probably never seen it."

"I see all kinds of movies, not just macho ones," Will defended himself.

"Wait a minute, now…" Jay was looking pleased with himself, "Does it have anything to do with what we are doing right now?"

Anne was confused for a second, and then noticed that Jay started waving his arms like an orchestra conductor, "Cliiimb everyyy mountaaain…" He had a decent singing voice.

"SOUND OF MUSIC," Will yelled, "Of, *course*."

"No *way*," Anne was shocked, "you've seen it?"

The guys were laughing and celebrating like children- with high-fives, and hip bumps.

"Come on, we both have mothers." Jay stated as if that alone was a plausible explanation.

"Were my children, by chance, climbing trees today?" Will added triumphantly.

"It got caught…in Friedrich's teeth," Jay said with his forefinger in the air and a German accent.

Anne was incredulous and had to laugh with them both. She was having fun.

They stopped to rest at the next switchback. They were considerably higher now, and could see where the others were a little further up at the top. They were not far from them; maybe two more switchbacks.

The view was breathtaking, especially since the eastern haze had disappeared. Anne thought about her chair.

As if Will knew what she was thinking he remarked, "I should have brought a chair for you."

She laughed and nodded, "I was just thinking that. I'm afraid that I am spoiled now, and the view from the house won't be enough anymore." She put her hands on her hips and then spread them out in front of her, "I need *this*."

They agreed and stood silently to take in the beauty that was before them.

After a few minutes, Jay's phone buzzed in the silence, and he shaded it with his hand so he could see the screen in the bright sun. "Rick says they are coming down, and to stay where we are."

Anne threw her hands in the air in celebration, "YAY, I don't think I can climb another step."

Will pulled his pack off and began digging in it for something. He came up with a bunch of bananas and handed one to each of them.

"Potassium. Perfect," Anne declared and almost immediately had half of hers eaten.

By the time the others arrived, the three of them had each eaten a banana, a protein bar, and were drinking a sports drink.

Lila bounded up to Anne and threw her arms around her, "Are you okay?"

"Yes, my girl, I am just fine," Anne hugged her back and then pulled away because they were both sweaty, "These two have been entertaining me and making sure I took my time." She indicated the vista, "Isn't this the best?"

Lila nodded and then whispered to Anne a little too loud, "Rick said he thought you wouldn't make it."

Anne looked over at Rick in reaction to this statement and he looked like he had been slapped. Lila probably wasn't supposed to share that little tidbit.

"Well, he was right, wasn't he?" Anne smiled to show it didn't bother her. It really didn't. She really had no business trying to climb this mountain. "I will already not be able to walk tomorrow, and I know that going down is even harder. Can I just slide down the sides?"

Henzie made the declaration that she was also worn out and would be going really slow down the trail. Anne handed her the last banana as the group started down.

Anne was correct. Down was worse than up. With every step, she thought her legs would give out. They were getting wiggly and she was becoming less and less confident that they would stay strong enough to make it down.

Henzie locked arms with Anne on one side and Chas on the other so they could support each other. Jay joined in and grabbed Anne's other arm and they successfully made it all the way down as one unit without any falls.

The other four were a little quicker getting down, but not by much. As they rounded the corner near the end of the trail, the rest of the group came into view. Lila was sitting on a rock that was about five feet tall and when she saw her sister, she got up to stand on the rock and waved.

What happened next would play in slow motion in Anne's memory forever.

Chapter 22

"LOOK HENZ," Lila lifted her left foot over her head with her left hand in standing splits and then said, "catch me," and jumped with her standing leg into a horizontal spin where both of her legs came together as she twisted in midair then began falling backwards into the waiting arms of her catcher. It would have been flawless if any of the three guys leaning against the rock had been ready. Rick had looked up a split second after she said, 'catch me,' but he was turned the wrong way and couldn't get his arms out in time. The forward motion of his arms thrown out too late pushed Lila's falling form toward the rock. Lila hit the rock pretty hard first with the side of her body and then with her head. It bounced against the rock and she started sliding. Rick was able to keep her from hitting the ground, but by then she was dead weight.

All Anne could hear was Henzie screaming as the four of them began running as best they could the final 50 feet to the bottom of the trail and Lila's lifeless body.

Anne guessed she was the only one with any medical knowledge, so she helped Rick lower her slowly to lie on the dirt in the shade of the rock. Luke was already on the phone to 911. Anne had not heard him speak with such confidence and determination until that moment. He knew exactly where they were, and knew Lila's full name, height, weight, and was pretty accurate in his assessment of her injuries. Anne was impressed.

Lila was breathing, but unconscious. Anne called to Lila and started asking if she could hear her and told her that everything would be okay. She felt Lila's limbs for broken bones. Anne then lifted Lila's legs to rest on one of the backpacks and asked the guys for their shirts so she could cover her and keep her from going into shock. Rick even had a sweatshirt in his pack.

Rick sat back against the rock holding his head and began mumbling something about not realizing she was going to do it again. "I told her not to do it anymore." He repeated that over and over until Jay got him up and walked him a little way away. Jay stood with Rick and tried to be comforting.

Chas was holding onto Henzie, who was sobbing into his shoulder and calling Lila's name as they both knelt next her injured twin. Will and Luke were pacing near the trail head looking out for the ambulance. Thankfully the trailhead parking lot could be seen from the highway.

Through tear-filled eyes, Anne wet one of the shirts with water and began carefully sponging

Lila's forehead and arms with the cool water while they waited for the ambulance. She grabbed Henzie's arm with her other hand and said gently, "Henz...honey..., you need to call your mom and dad."

Chas got the hint and took over, "Come on babe, you have to be brave for Lila. We need to call your parents. Where is your phone?"

Henzie took off her pack and found her phone in the front pocket. She hit the home button and said in a shaky voice, "Call mom," and the phone did the rest.

As soon as she said, "Mamma?" she started crying again at the sound of her mom's voice. Chas took the phone and began explaining what had just happened.

Anne was startled when Chas said, "Yes, Anne is right here," and handed her Henzie's phone.

"Hello," Anne said in her calmest, steadiest voice. She didn't want to panic June Musgrove. Chas had done well so far and June was not hysterical.

"Anne dear, can you tell me what happened in your nurse voice?" June requested. Her voice sounded calm, but emotional as expected.

Anne explained in detail what had happened and a little about what Lila had been doing up until that last jump, and then added, "I don't think anything is broken, but she hit her head pretty hard, and she is not conscious at the moment. I've got her feet elevated and I am watching that she doesn't go into shock. We are waiting for the ambulance."

"Can I ask you to stay with my daughters until

we can get there?"

"Of course, I will."

"Can you let Rick know that this was not his fault," June said with emotion. "I don't want that boy to blame himself for my daughter's flights of fancy."

"I will tell him that, but he may not listen. He is already feeling responsible."

"Then I will tell him myself!" June declared, "Give him the phone, and then I will continue to talk to you, so don't hang up."

Anne got up, which was difficult because her muscles were screaming, and hobbled over to Rick with the phone. He looked miserable, and she, like June, wanted him to realize that this accident was not his fault. Lila had done this to herself. As harsh as that sounded at the moment, there was nothing anyone could have done to prevent her from jumping off that rock when she did.

Anne looked up at Rick and put one hand on his arm and squeezed it to get his attention. She held the phone out and said, "Rick, Lila's mom wants to say something to you."

He looked afraid, but his expression changed when he looked into Anne's eyes and saw immediately what she was thinking. She was trying to convey that there was no judgement or criticism; only love and compassion in the message.

He took the phone and looked at his feet, "Hello, June, I'm so sorry."

Anne was standing close enough to Rick to hear June clearly, "Now, you listen to me good...you are not to blame for this...you hear me?" She must have been yelling into the phone for effect.

Rick nodded and mumbled. He was looking everywhere but at Anne; up the mountain, over at Lila, off into space, but Anne never took her eyes off of his face. She wanted to make sure that when he did look at her, she was there for him. She wanted to wrap her arms around him, and figured if she did, it would not seem inappropriate in this situation. She just needed the courage.

June continued, "Don't you dare spend one moment saying 'if only'…My daughter is impulsive and thoughtless and does these things to herself. Your only *fault* is being a gentleman. And that is not a fault."

Rick nodded again and managed to be coherent in his reply, "Thank you." His voice was full of emotion.

June's voice got a little quieter and Anne couldn't make out what she said next, but whatever it was, Rick looked right at her and nodded again and said confidently, "I was already going to make sure that happened."

He listened a few seconds with his eyes still on Anne, and then handed her the phone. As she took it from him, their fingers touched and that did it. He pulled her into his arms and she melted into him. She wrapped her arms around his waist and held him tightly. He rested his cheek against her head and she felt him take a deep breath and let it out slowly. He still had his shirt on because she had used his sweatshirt to cover Lila, and he was not as sweaty as she was. She started to feel self-conscious that she was less than fresh, but he wasn't letting go, and neither was she. She could feel his body slowly relax and melt into hers. She was becoming intoxicated with his smell and didn't want to let go.

After what seemed like many minutes, she could hear June calling her name from the phone in her hand, and a far-off ambulance siren getting closer.

At the reality of those sounds, Rick suddenly let her go, and turned to join Will and Luke at the trailhead, without another look.

She stood there for a second and started shaking from the sudden lack of support. She frantically looked for a place to sit down so she wouldn't collapse. Jay had been right there next to them, and was a little baffled by Rick's quick departure. He was able to grab Anne as her legs buckled under her.

She held the phone to her ear and let June know she was there as Jay half carried her over to a smaller rock so she could sit. She listened to June give her details of their plan to get there as soon as possible. Anne was only half listening at this point, overwhelmed with Rick's hug on top of all that was happening, but she was able to get the gist of what to expect the next day. Someone needed to pick them up at Burbank airport at some point and June would let Henzie know the details later.

She ended the call and wanted to go back to Lila, but didn't think she could move. She took a minute to take everything in. The adrenaline that had carried her for the last few minutes was gone. She was exhausted and shaky and starting to feel dizzy and chilled. It was at least 80 degrees where they were, so she shouldn't be cold. She shook off the idea that she may, herself, be going into shock, and took some slow, deep breaths with her head down until she started to feel better.

Jay fetched the backpack she had set down near where Lila was laying, as the ambulance pulled up into the small parking lot. She drank what was left of her sports drink and took some ibuprofen that she had thrown in the pack for this very reason.

She sat helpless and watched as the paramedics rolled a stretcher over to Lila and knelt by her body to assess her injuries. They immobilized her neck in a collar and strapped her to a backboard before putting her on the stretcher. She saw Jay say something to one of the medics and they came over and asked her some questions about her own symptoms. She answered in medical terms what she was feeling and they gave her some instructions for later that she was planning on doing anyway, and gave her a thumbs up.

Jay was there with her the whole time and after her encounter with the medics he said, "Are you a doctor or something?"

She laughed a little, "No. I was in the nursing program in college. That's all."

"That's all?" Jay was smiling, "You sounded like a doctor just now."

Before she could comment further, Rick was standing over her all of a sudden holding out his hand to help her stand up.

"Come on, you are going with the girls in the ambulance."

"What?" She was surprised. She figured Chas and Henzie would go, or just Henzie.

"The medics say they have room for two and I promised June that you would stay with her girls." Rick was practically picking her up and she had to shake free of him and push him away.

"I can walk, dang it," She took a few steps, felt dizzy, and stopped to steady herself. Maybe not?

She scolded Rick, "You made me stand up too quickly." She took another step but didn't get very far.

Rick leaned toward her, grabbed her arm and swung it over his head as he bent and picked her up effortlessly and carried her the 20 feet to the ambulance. For a second, his seriousness disappeared and he grinned at her just before depositing her into the back of the ambulance. Butterflies were fluttering inside her.

As he set her down, she smiled back and messed up his hair, "Show off."

He nodded with an eyebrow raised. The old Rick. More butterflies.

"I'll bring you some fresh clothes, but take this for now," Rick handed her his backpack and took her hand and squeezed it before he backed up so they could shut the door and get moving.

She watched him through the back window as the ambulance pulled away. He never took his eyes off of her until they were out of sight.

Chapter 23

Anne and Henzie were sitting in a waiting area in the Emergency Room.

They had been there for 20 minutes and no one had come to talk to them. Anne had her right arm around Henzie as the twin sat with her head in her hands. She was done crying. She had cried nonstop since the accident. Anne had cried, too. The reality that Lila hadn't woken up in the ambulance was frightening. Anne knew that this meant that Lila's brain was injured, and that was never good. They could only hope and pray that she would wake up soon.

The ibuprofen had kicked in and Anne was feeling a little less wiped out, and she was no longer experiencing bouts of dizziness.

Henzie sat up straight and turned to give Anne a hug. They held onto each other for about a minute and then Henzie pulled away and asked where the bathroom was.

While Henzie was in the bathroom, Anne absently opened the pack that Rick had given her when he put her in the ambulance. It contained his sweatshirt, which she promptly put on. It was cold in the hospital. How thoughtful of him. And—bonus—it smelled like him. She snuggled into it and brought the hood up around her neck and brought the fabric up to her face closed her eyes and took a deep breath. Mmmmm. She thought about how it had felt when he picked her up and then grinned at her, and the butterflies came back.

The pack also contained three protein bars, and apple, and two sports drinks. She had eaten all the food in her pack on the mountain, and was feeling like she should be eating something.

She ate one of the protein bars before Henzie returned. Henzie had washed her face, so she looked less like a refugee with smeared dirt and tears. Anne held out a protein bar and Henzie accepted it gladly and tore into it.

"Thank you," Henzie spoke with a mouthful, "I am not hungry *at all*, but I know I need to eat something."

Anne reached out and pushed Henzie's hair behind her ear, "You look much better."

"I wish they would come tell us what is going on."

"I know," Anne agreed, "but we can take comfort in the fact that if they aren't out here talking to us, they are in there helping Lila."

"True. I hadn't thought of that."

There was a commotion by the automatic doors to the outside and suddenly the girls were joined by all the guys, and everyone started talking at once. Henzie jumped up and ran into Chas's arms, and Will sat by Anne, full of questions. Rick hung back with Luke and sat in seats across from Anne. She didn't see Jay.

Anne tried to answer all the questions, but she really did not have any new information.

She noticed that Rick was holding her purse and another bag from the house. She was hoping it was a change of clothes for her and Henzie.

When the questions turned into silence, Rick spoke up, "We brought you both a change of clothes and your purses."

Anne thanked him, stood up, and took the bag and her purse and excused herself to go change in the restroom. She was curious to see what clothes she would find in the bag. He had been in her room, obviously, and gone through her things. She tried not to think about the awkwardness of *that* whole situation. What did he choose?

There was an unfamiliar outfit on top, which she set aside as Henzie's. Under that was the blue button-down shirt with the little flowers she had worn to Mary's for that dinner when Rick showed up while she was hiding in the bathroom... the first time they had seen each other in ten years.

What? Was this a coincidence?

He had also included her jeans. She was dying in the cold hospital and was beyond grateful for the warm denim. There was also a sweatshirt, but she chose to leave that in the bag and put his sweatshirt back on after she had changed. She hoped he would notice.

She gave herself a quick sponge bath with some wet paper towels and washed off all the dirt and sweat. She discovered he had also included her deodorant and some lotion in her purse, so she used them and felt relatively clean and fresh again. He had thought of everything.

"Anne?" Henzie entered the bathroom just as Anne was putting her shoes back on with clean socks, and she handed the bag over the stall door so Henzie could clean up as well.

"Good grief, they remembered everything?" Henzie said from inside her stall, "These are guys. They are not supposed to be thoughtful like this, right?"

"The good ones are," Anne said with a smile, and then had a thought. "Where is Jay? I didn't see him. Was he parking the car?"

"Oh…no…he stayed at the house to wait for his wife. She was almost there, but Rick didn't want to wait for her."

Sarah.

Chapter 24

When Anne emerged from the bathroom, she looked very different. She had removed her baseball cap and braided her hair, and was dressed in her jeans and blue shirt, with Rick's sweatshirt on, but unzipped.

She stole a glance at Rick to see if he noticed she still had his sweatshirt on, and he was staring, but when she caught his eye, he looked away.

Okay?

She was completely unable to predict how he was going to act, and was annoyed by that.

She sat down where she had been sitting before, right next to Will, but across from Rick. It seemed expected. She would have rather sat next to Rick, but wasn't sure what he was thinking at this point, and was aware of how it might look to the others if she suddenly changed spots. If they were even paying attention at this point...

"Did the doctor come out while I was

changing?" She asked the room as she took her seat.

Everyone said "no" in unison, and it was quiet for a while. Will and Chas were looking at their phones, and Rick was staring into space. Luke was pacing a little way away. *He's taking this harder than I expected*, Anne thought. Then she remembered that his fiancée had died in an accident. *Good grief, this is probably agonizing for him. He should have stayed at the house.*

She leaned forward to get Rick's attention and said in a whisper, "Is Luke okay? I mean...should he be here? He is depressed enough to have to endure waiting around in a hospital..."

Rick nodded and looked around at Luke, then turned back and shrugged his shoulders, "Jay asked. But he insisted on coming."

Anne raised her eyebrows and sat back in her seat.

"How are you feeling now, Anne?" Will asked without looking up from his phone, "Are you still hurting from the hike?"

"I'm doing pretty well. I took about 80 ibuprofen an hour ago when we first arrived, so it's taken the edge off. I expect I'll be sore tomorrow."

He looked up surprised when she said "80 ibuprofen" but then recognized she was exaggerating and returned to his phone.

"Did you just down the whole bottle?" Rick laughed, and when she laughed as well, he looked over at Will.

"I wanted to. I don't think I've ever been this wiped out."

Rick kept looking at Will, who was still on his

phone. She wanted to wave her hands and scream, *Hello! I'm right here, look at me. I'm the one speaking.*

Henzie emerged from the restroom and sat next to Chas. He put his arm around her and she rested her head on his shoulder.

Anne wanted to lie down. The chairs were adequately comfortable, but not for the state her body was in. She kept looking at the floor and wondering if it would be horribly inappropriate for her to just curl up on the floor in the space over by the window.

Before she could think any more about it, three doctors walked through the double doors and one said, "Who is here for Lila Musgrove?"

They all stood up and Henzie practically ran over to them, "I'm her twin…" She looked back and pointed at Anne, "and that is our…my other sister, Anne."

Anne almost objected instinctively, but Rick put his hand on her back and propelled her forward in support of what Henzie said. She remembered what he had promised June.

She walked forward. They were only going to give important information to family, and she knew that Henzie was too emotional to remember anything, so she stuck her hand out and shook the lead doctor's hand after Henzie had. Henzie then grabbed Anne's hand in a death grip.

The doctors explained that Lila was in a medically induced coma. She had sustained an injury to her brain. The MRI had shown massive swelling and she needed to remain in the hospital until the swelling went down. In all other respects she was unhurt. Just a swollen bump on her head and some bruises to her torso. The older doctor then explained that they were going to keep her in a coma overnight, and then see if anything changed in the morning.

Henzie slumped into Chas and started crying softly. Anne stood quietly alone.

Two of the doctors left and the remaining doctor stayed to reassure both women that they were doing all they could to keep Lila comfortable and that she was expected to recover once the swelling went down, but it was still a waiting game, and there were no guarantees.

He also said that only one person was allowed to stay with Lila in her room overnight. And it would be a few hours until she was transferred to a room and could have any visitors, so there would be no reason to wait around in the hospital. He suggested the group go eat somewhere and if someone was going to stay overnight, to come back at seven.

He left them and went back through the double doors.

Chapter 25

They all walked absently out to the car, and when they got there, someone realized that they didn't have enough seats in the car. They were going to have to wait for Jay.

As they were standing at the car, Anne discovered that she was going to either have to sit down or fall down. She kept this to herself, because she didn't want to make a fuss, so she looked around and there was a bench close by, on a walkway that jutted out from the doors to the hospital into the parking lot. She made her way over to the bench and sat down. When she looked back at the car, she realized that no one had seen her move. *We are all a sorry bunch*, she thought.

They were all looking around for Jay's car. She rested her arm on the back of the bench and laid her head on her arm. She closed her eyes and took some deep breaths.

"Are you okay?" Will's voice was close to her

head and she felt him sit down beside her on the bench.

She didn't open her eyes because it felt too good, "I just need to sit. I don't think I can stand for very long. I've had it."

"We will just wait here until the others decide what to do."

She nodded. "Hmmm," and they sat there for a few minutes, and she could feel herself getting sleepy in the warm sun.

Rick's voice sounded far away, "You take them home, and when Jay gets here, Luke and I will go with him and we will grab some food and bring it to the house on our way." And that was all she heard before she fell asleep.

She was slightly aware of being lifted and then set down gently onto something soft and comfortable. She couldn't wake herself up, so she gave in.

* * *

"She's been asleep for hours, should we wake her so she can eat?"

Anne felt a hand on her arm and opened her eyes to see Sarah smiling down at her. She was lying on the sofa in Jay's great room and she could smell garlic. She was suddenly starving.

She sat up and Sarah sat beside her and wrapped her in a big hug.

"Oh my gosh, Sarah," Anne held her tight, "It is so good to see you."

"You too, my friend," Sarah pulled away and

looked at her, "You have had quite a day, I hear."

"That is the understatement of the century."

"No doubt."

"How long have I been asleep and how the heck did I get here?

Will answered from the kitchen, "You have been out for about three hours. I put you in the car and then carried you from the car to the sofa. First class transportation."

"I'm sorry," Anne turned to look at him, and found him walking toward her with a plate full of pasta with a big meatball in the center.

"Your dinner, Milady," He bowed and handed her the plate and she started eating like she had never seen food before.

She said, "thank you," between bites. He returned to the kitchen to fetch a plate of garlic knots and a drink.

She finished the pasta pretty quickly and started on the garlic knots.

"These are delicious. Where is everyone? Aren't you going to eat?"

Will laughed. "Slow down, girl. We ate two hours ago. I just heated that up for you." He took the empty plate from her and set it on the ottoman. "Let's see…locations…Chas drove Henzie to the hospital, like, and hour ago. He isn't back yet. Jay and Luke are downstairs doing who knows what, and Rick is gone."

She stopped chewing and she felt like she'd been punched in the stomach. "Gone?...Where did he go?" she tried not to look panicked.

"Home," Sarah stated matter-of-factly, but the

incredulous look on Anne's face made her feel like she needed to elaborate. "He is picking up Lila's parents tomorrow morning early at the Burbank Airport, and he lives relatively close to the airport so he thought it would be easier to sleep in his own bed and not have to get up as early in the morning and drive all the way from here in traffic."

Anne nodded, and her heart started beating again. She had missed a lot while she was "out." She hoped Sarah and Will had not noticed her panic just then.

"Well, if you girls don't need anything from me, I'm wasted, and going to bed."

"Thank you, Will," Sarah smiled and nodded, "Thank you for taking such good care of my friend."

"At your sehveece mon cherees," Will replied in his best French accent as he bowed, and then disappeared around the corner.

"Okay, girl," Sarah turned toward her on the sofa, "What is going on? I know you. We may not have seen each other much in the last 11 years, but we were inseparable in college and you can't have changed *that* much...spill."

"Before I say anything, I have to know what happened with Rick introducing you to Jay...What was said? How did it happen?"

"Really?"

"Please... Tell me that, and then I will tell you all that has happened to me in these last three crazy weeks."

"Well, first off, who told you about it? Rick, or Jay?"

"Rick."

"Okay," Sarah laughed a little and then told Anne that six years ago she had been scheduled to meet and interview two entrepreneur software designers who had insisted on being interviewed together because they were pals and their products were complimentary. It would benefit both to be featured together, and it just made marketing sense. Rick developed the games, and Jay developed the equipment and accompanying software that provided the best gaming experience for those games. She had no objection and agreed with them.

"When I walked into the building, I had no idea that the 'Rick Wentworth' I was meeting was *your* Rick Wentworth, or I may have cancelled the interview. I walked in and there he was. Jay was late, and Rick shook my hand and started to explain why Jay wasn't there, and then stopped and really looked at me. He said my name again, but this time it was a question, and I told him that, yes, he was correct, I was *your* Sarah Smith. He turned red and didn't let go of my hand, and asked about you: how you were, where you were, and all that. He was very intense. He finally let go of my hand and we sat down while I tried to give him accurate information about you. I believe at that time you were at home and keeping house for your father and sister. I told him that I didn't hear from you that often because you were not big on social media.

He asked if you were a nurse, and I told him that I didn't think so, but that didn't really mean anything since I hadn't kept in touch like I should have." She looked down at her hands.

"Oh, come on, I'm just as much to blame, keep going."

Sarah went on to explain that at that point she had told him what she thought of how he had ended things with Anne. "I really let him have it."

"That is what he told me."

"Good." Sarah looked satisfied, "And I keep telling him each time I see him, which is quite often since he and Jay are best friends and work together in the same building."

"What?" Anne laughed out loud, "You are kidding, right? You keep reminding him? That often?" She gave Sarah a high five. "Go Sarah."

"And he generally agrees with me each time."

Anne's eyes grew wide. "Really?"

"Yes," Sarah nodded, "Sometimes I think he does that to get me to stop, but other times I believe he really thinks so."

"Does he date?" Anne was afraid to hear the answer to this, but had to ask.

Sarah shook her head. "Not really. He has gone out with a few different women in the last few years, but none that last longer than a few dates."

"I have been trying to figure out how we got thrown together for the last three weeks."

Sarah leaned back into the sofa cushions, "I just know that Jay told me that Rick was going to visit his sister in her new place, and when Jay asked Rick where it was, Rick mentioned the city where I knew you lived. Did he know where you lived?"

"He had never been there, but he knew the street and the city because he used to make fun of it, and declare that he couldn't possibly live up to the idyllic sound of my address in a million years. I had forgotten all about that until last week."

"Well, I agree. Paradise Lane in Eden Grove is a crazy address."

"He had to know that his sister had either purchased my house, or one on my street."

"So…" Sarah adjusted her position on the sofa, "Spill it. I told you what I know. What's been going on?"

Anne began with her horror when she read the names on the real estate purchase contract, explained what had gone on at the lake house and here at the beach, and ended with Rick picking her up and carrying her over to the ambulance.

"And he still hasn't said one word to me or anyone else about our almost-engagement."

"Wow." Sarah was unable to say anything else. Both women relaxed back into the sofa cushions lost in thought.

After a few minutes of silence, Anne got up and refilled her drink. She was sore and it was hard to move. When she returned to the sofa Sarah finally said, "I can't believe he hasn't said anything to you."

"He has been acting like we had only just met two weeks ago, presumably because he assumes that no one else knows about our previous relationship. The only time he was remotely familiar with me was when we were on the beach yesterday morning. It was just the two of us, and it was only for about five minutes. He seemed like he was about to talk about it when we heard the others coming down the stairs. And then, earlier today when he picked me up and put me in the ambulance, he seemed like the old Rick."

"Do you think he is serious about Lila?" Sarah said as she screwed up her face in disapproval.

"He is paying her a lot of attention, but I don't know if that is just because she is demanding it, and he is just being nice? Or if he really wants to."

"I don't see them really fitting." Sarah shook her head, "She is way too young. And not just because she is actually, what? 10 years younger than him? But because, from what I am hearing, she acts a whole lot younger than him. I mean, what's with the cheerleading moves? Really now."

Anne agreed, "Yes, I have been wondering that, too. But I thought I was a tad biased."

"Do you still have feelings for him?"

Anne lowered her head and looked at her drink. "I never stopped."

"Oh sweetie." Sarah sat up and put her arm around Anne for a few moments, "I was going to ask you about Will."

"What about him?"

Sarah laughed and sat back, "Jay said that Will has been paying you a lot of attention for the last two days."

"Oh, yes he has," Anne smiled. "It feels good to be admired, but I have already talked to him and told him that I wasn't interested. He seemed to be relieved. It was almost like he thought I expected him to chase me. He is nice, but is a little too full of himself."

"I know," Sarah rolled her eyes, "he's one of those guys who thinks all women swoon over him. I mean, he's gorgeous and all, but good grief. The whole world does not revolve around him. He has been a good distraction for Luke, though. Even though I think he has taken advantage of his cousin a little too long."

The front door opened and Chas walked in. He gave them an update on Lila's condition. She was still in a coma, but was stable and Henzie was with her, talking to her. One of the nurses told them that she believed that coma patients can hear what is going on around them, so it was important to be positive and act like Lila was aware. This was all Henzie needed to hear. She was going to talk to Lila and tell her stories and sing to her.

He also told them that the Musgroves would be there early in the morning. Rick was going to take them straight to the hospital and then return to the beach house.

Chas said goodnight and disappeared down the stairs to his room.

"I'm not sure what to do now," Anne said as she stood up to say goodnight.

"What do you mean?" Sarah stood up as well.

"Well, it seems wrong to stay here once Lila's parents get here." Anne gave Sarah a hug. "I should see about going home."

"No way," Sarah chided, "You are staying here to make sure Lila will be okay, and then after a few days, I will take you home. You are not leaving me here with all these guys."

Chapter 26

Anne woke to the sound of a car door. She rolled over and grabbed her phone to see what time it was. 9:22. She had slept over 12 hours. Her muscles felt a little sore, but not in a bad way. She was no longer fatigued and exhausted.

She stretched out on the bed, and then got up and stretched the muscles in her legs and arms. She was glad that she had eaten that banana and downed those ibuprofen tablets. She wasn't as sore as she had anticipated.

Curious about the car door, she looked out her window. Since her room faced the front of the house she could see a new car next to Henzie's. It was a sleek, black, M85 BMW. She had never seen one like it before. Fancy. As she wondered whose it was, she saw Chas and Luke emerge from the front door, get in Henzie's car and drive away.

They must be going to the hospital, she thought to herself, *I need to be going there myself.* She quickly showered and got dressed, and went out to the kitchen to get some breakfast.

Will was sitting at the table eating a piece of toast and scrambled eggs. "There are eggs in the skillet if you're interested," he said with a mouthful of toast.

"Thank you," Anne dished herself some eggs and put a piece of toast in the toaster. As she waited for her toast, she took a bite of the eggs, "Mmmm, these are good, thank you for making them."

"Nope, not me." Will answered with yet another mouthful of food, "They were here when I came up a few minutes ago." He waved his fork around in thought, "Maybe Rick made them. He got here a little bit ago, and Jay and Sarah went out walking around 9, so they couldn't have. They are still warm."

Anne's mind went immediately back to a time when Rick made eggs for her once after a date. They had tasted just like this.

"Did Chas and Luke go to the hospital?"

"I think so," Will scooped up the last of his eggs with a flourish and practically swallowed them whole. He stood and took his plate to the sink and set it there for someone else to put in the dishwasher. He turned to Anne with a dazzling smile and announced that he was going down to the beach.

"Wanna join me?"

Anne must have looked as shocked as she felt because he stopped and put his hands on his hips— clearly perplexed.

"What?"

She collected herself before replying as calmly as possible, "I don't think I can sit on a beach while my friend is in a coma."

"Oh, yeah, that." He shrugged his shoulders and left her standing in the kitchen as her toast popped up.

What a jerk. Completely self-absorbed. It's like yesterday never happened.

As she continued to think of creative adjectives to describe him while she finished her breakfast, Sarah and Jay came through the door and joined her in the kitchen.

"Rick is back?" Jay asked Anne.

"I don't know," Anne shrugged, even though she knew that he had to have made the eggs.

"Sorry," Jay laughed, "that was more of a statement. His car is outside."

"Wait a minute," Anne looked puzzled, "If his car is outside, how did he get to his house last night?"

Sarah explained, "I believe he used a ride-share to get home yesterday."

Anne nodded. That made sense.

"Are you feeling better today?" Sarah asked Anne.

"Oh yes. I believe I am back to normal. I am just a little sore—but less than I imagined I would be."

"Fantastic," Jay smiled and grabbed Sarah's hand, "We are going to get ready to go to the hospital. Do you want to ride with us? We will be ready in, what? 30 minutes?" He looked at Sarah for confirmation.

Sarah nodded, and they both left the room hand

in hand.

Anne went to the window that looked out on the driveway. *Rick must really be doing well to drive one of those*, she thought as she looked the black sports sedan. He always liked the German cars.

She went back into the kitchen and cleaned up the dishes that were there. Actually, it was only hers and Will's dishes, and the skillet. When she was done, she went back to her room to brush her teeth and put on shoes. She grabbed her purse and went back into the front room to wait for Jay and Sarah. *Maybe Rick would come with them*, she thought as she waited on "her" chair by the window. The water was so blue in the morning light. There was a trio of kayaks out about 100 yards making their way west, and she could see Will swimming closer to shore. She shook her head. She still couldn't figure him out. Luke had gone with Chas to the hospital. That showed true compassion and empathy for the family. Luke had first-hand knowledge of what it was like to grieve for a loved one in the hospital after an accident. Will had no clue, or he didn't care. The more she thought about it, the more perturbed she became.

She shook her head again, this time to shake the angry thoughts out of her head. She had to stay positive and upbeat, for Lila, and the Musgroves.

Sarah and Jay took a little longer than 30 minutes, but when they came up the stairs, they brought with them some news from the hospital.

"Luke just texted me that the doctors decided to keep Lila in a coma for another day so that the swelling in her brain could have more time to lessen." Jay said.

"But we are still going over there to support the family and bring them breakfast," Sarah announced, "We are going to stop at our favorite place and grab breakfast burritos for all of them."

Anne decided it wouldn't be weird to ask, "Is Rick coming?"

Jay shook his head, "That boy is tired from all the driving. He is asleep. He texted me earlier that he was going to get some sleep and then meet us over there later."

Anne caught Sarah's eye and Sarah winked. Anne turned red, but Jay was oblivious as he opened the garage and pulled his car out. It was identical to Rick's but in red.

"Did you get matching cars on purpose?" Anne laughed as she squeezed into the backseat.

It was Sarah's turn to laugh. "They went to the dealership together after their first quarter earnings."

Jay was laughing too. "Come on girls, it's a guy thing."

"At least they aren't the same color," Anne said as she laughed.

"That would be a girl thing," Jay added.

"Not even," Sarah argued playfully. "I would never buy a matching car even if I was a twin."

At the word "twin" the three in the car got quiet, and were silent until they got to the burrito place.

Chapter 27

Anne was sitting in the waiting room at the hospital holding the bag of burritos. She had let Jay and Sarah go into Lila's room first. They were only allowing four visitors at a time. The room wasn't very big, so even four felt crowded according to Luke.

Henzie and Chas had gone back to the house so that she could shower and change clothes. They had taken their burritos with them.

Luke sat across from Anne. He was like a different person. He was no longer brooding and sullen. He had perked up somehow. Anne could not account for the change. It seemed to her that the opposite should have happened. Being in this hospital should have made his sadness over the loss of his fiancé even deeper, but it hadn't.

He was eating his burrito and looking out the window.

"Tell me again what the doctor said about

keeping her in the coma," She asked Luke.

Between bites, he explained that when he and Chas had arrived earlier, the doctors were talking to the Musgroves and giving them the option of weaning Lila off the drugs that were keeping her in a coma. They explained that the longer she was kept in a coma, the more time her brain had for the swelling to go down. But, the longer she was in a coma, the less likely she would be able to come out of it. It was a fine line, and the doctors wanted to make sure the family was informed of all the risks and benefits.

Landry and June had decided to keep her in a coma one more day and then wean her off the drugs and see if she wakes up. Even though it was agonizing to see her in a coma, they thought it was wise to give the swelling in her brain a chance to subside first.

Luke said all of this with hope and optimism, which surprised Anne. He even smiled. She thought she would ask the obvious since he seemed so content.

"Isn't it hard to be in a hospital after what happened to your fiancé?"

Luke looked thoughtful for a moment and Anne hoped that she hadn't jinxed it by bringing it up.

"Actually, I thought it would be bad, but Lila's prognosis is so much different than Cassie's," he said with conviction, "Cassie was immediately in surgery and we waited on edge for almost three hours, and then were told that she didn't make it. I am feeling very differently about Lila. She is still alive a whole day later. It has to be a good sign. At least that is how I feel."

"Well, you are very kind to wait with us," Anne was touched by his dedication having known Lila only two days.

"Of course. Where else would I be?" He said matter-of-factly. "Where is Will, by the way?"

"He…" She wasn't sure how to tell him where his cousin was, "He is at the beach."

"Naturally…" Luke shook his head slightly, "…my cousin…well…he is an only child…I wonder if that explains anything?"

Anne smiled. She was glad to see that he knew his own cousin. "I think so."

Jay and Sarah emerged from the double doors to the ICU wing and indicated that she should go in, and take the burritos to the Musgroves.

June enveloped her in a big hug when she walked through the door to Lila's room, and held her for multiple minutes. Landry joined in the hug and Anne was completely surrounded by a loving embrace. The tenderness made her cry. These people who had loved her through the years like their own daughter were hurting and she was so glad to be able to be there for them.

When they finally backed away, June was wiping her eyes along with Anne.

"Well, my dear," June began, "I think it was wise for you to be here to be the level head during all this commotion."

"What do you mean?" Anne asked.

"Well, Rick went on and on about how calm and collected you were after Lila fell, and how you took over like a professional," Landry said proudly, "We have you to thank for her being in such good condition.

"Yes, the doctors said it could have been worse, and praised her care before the ambulance arrived." June beamed, and took Anne's face in her hands, "You saved our girl."

"Oh, my, no," Anne was embarrassed. "I didn't do all that much."

June wagged her finger in Anne's face, "Nonsense, child, you used your training. No one else knew what to do. I'm so proud of you. Thank you." And she grabbed Anne in another bear hug.

After the second, shorter hug, Anne handed them their burritos and both sat down to eat them after thanking her. Anne went over to Lila and took her hand. She leaned down and kissed her cheek and whispered that she would be okay and that they were all there looking after her. She spent the next few minutes telling Lila what the weather was like outside, and how Rick had gone to get her parents, and how the beach had looked that morning. She was trying to think of things to say, so that if Lila could hear her, it would mean something.

June interrupted her, "Tell me about this boy, Luke."

"Luke?" Anne looked up at June, surprised at the question.

"Yes, he seems like a nice, steady, thoughtful young man."

"Well, let's see," Anne began, unsure why June was asking, "He was engaged to Jay's sister, Cassie, last year when she was in a car accident and was killed."

"Oh my stars! How awful for both of them."

"Yes indeed," Anne nodded sadly. "I asked him a moment ago, before I came back here, how he was doing with being in such a similar situation here in another hospital, and he assured me that this experience was vastly different than before..."

"I noticed that his demeanor has changed since yesterday. When we arrived two days ago, he was sullen and sad. He didn't talk hardly at all, and kept to himself even though he was with the group at the beach and at the boardwalk and pier. And when we hiked yesterday, he was with the twins and Chas and Rick. Jay and Will stayed back with me. I was sadly out of shape and unable to keep up with the younger, more fit members of the group." Anne smiled weakly.

"Who is Will?" Landry asked.

"Yes, we have not met him yet," June said, "Is he out in the lobby?"

"Will is Luke's cousin from Kansas," Anne said, "And, no, he is still back at the house." There was no way she was going to tell them that he had chosen to go swimming instead of coming to the hospital.

"Oh yes," June remembered, "Rick said something about him staying with his cousin while he tried to break into acting."

"Yes." Anne was unwilling to elaborate more on Will.

Landry asked, "Anne, dear, do you think we did the right thing letting her stay in the coma for another day? The doctor said there was no guarantee either way."

"Everything we were taught about brain injury in school, was always couched in uncertainty." Anne mused. "The brain is a mystery, but letting the swelling go down is a good thing. It always depends on the individual, and the situation."

Landry hugged Anne and June took Anne's hand, "We are so glad you are here," they both said almost in unison, and then June added, "I have been praying, and I just have a calm feeling that everything will be okay."

They stayed with Lila until lunch when Jay offered to go grab something and bring it back for everyone, and Anne and Sarah went with him. Henzie and Chas had returned by then and took over sitting with Lila and the Musgroves. Henzie was having a harder time than the rest of them. Because she was Lila's twin, she felt the void more keenly and claimed to be feeling sleepy and sluggish, almost like she was feeling the same things Lila was feeling.

"I just don't have any energy. It is really weird." Henzie would keep saying. "I've never felt this way before."

Anne had asked Luke if he wanted to come with them to get lunch, and he told her he preferred to stay at the hospital. She and Sarah had shared a look.

"He is really taking this in stride," Jay said as they got in the car.

"I am really surprised that he wants to stay at the hospital," Sarah remarked.

Anne told them what Luke said when she had asked him earlier about how he was feeling, and then she had a thought, "How are you both doing with this?"

Jay answered, "I'm a little freaked. I'll admit this isn't easy. It was a blow to everyone when the doctor came out and told us Cassie had died, and I've been having flashbacks of that day."

Sarah agreed and squeezed Jay's arm, "Me, too." She looked at Jay and then out the front window. "We talked it out on our walk this morning. Luke didn't speak for at least a week after Cassie died. I'm sure it is encouraging to him that Lila is still alive. But what is his motive here? He seems to be acting more like a boyfriend than an acquaintance."

"I know, right?" Jay said as he pulled the car out onto the street.

"Do you think that he likes Lila?" Anne decided to offer.

No one said anything, and rode, deep in thought to the burger place.

Chapter 28

All the young people were back at the beach house after spending the entire day at the hospital. Lila's mom and dad had decided to stay with her overnight.

Will had stayed on the beach all day, and Rick had slept until lunch and joined the group at the hospital just after that. He kept his distance from Anne while at the hospital and Anne could not account for his behavior. He wouldn't look in her direction, and after all of his attention the day before, she was feeling lost.

Luke and Rick had gone straight to their rooms when they arrived, and Chas and Henzie had gone off to take a walk on the beach to just be outside in the fresh air.

Anne sat in her chair and watched the sunset, while Sarah and Jay started making cookies in the kitchen.

"Oh geez," Sarah said suddenly, "Will left.

There is a note right here on the counter."

Anne turned to look at Sarah.

Jay started laughing, "He got an audition, so he's gone."

Anne couldn't help but be relieved. His behavior had been bothering her, and now she could relax and not worry about explaining his absence to June and Landry. She threw her fist in the air with a soft, "Whoo hooo," almost to herself.

"What?" Jay looked confused, and Sarah whispered something to him that Anne couldn't hear. "Oh."

Anne sat comfortably in her chair as the sun set in the western sky. With no clouds or haze today, the sunset was just okay. Not brilliant like that first night. She was just enjoying the ocean and the fading light when Rick came up the stairs with his suitcase. She tried not to look surprised, but she failed.

"I've got to get back to work," he mumbled to her as he passed her on his way into the kitchen. He didn't even give her a chance to say anything, and as he entered the kitchen, he began thanking the Harvilles for their hospitality and explaining that he felt like with the current circumstances, he should leave and get back to work.

Jay tried, "At least stay for cookies. We just put a tray in the oven. You are going to hit traffic."

"Thanks, but I think I need to just go."

"Okay, man." Jay came around the island and gave him a handshake/hug, "I'll be back in on Monday, if anyone asks."

And he was gone. He hadn't even turned around

to say goodbye to Anne. He just nodded to Sarah and walked out the door.

Anne heard his car start and then nothing, as a tear crept down her cheek. What had happened since yesterday? He had at least spoken with her yesterday and been thoughtful and attentive to her after Lila's accident. What was going on?

Sarah came over with two spoons full of cookie dough, handed Anne one of the spoons and sat in the other chair. "What was all that? He didn't even look at you?"

Anne took a mouthful of dough and closed her eyes, "I have no clue." She wiped the tear from her cheek and looked straight at Sarah. "I have absolutely no explanation."

"I'm so sorry." Sarah reached out and squeezed Anne's arm.

"Hey, babe," Jay called from the kitchen, "I offered the Musgroves a room here, but they booked a hotel closer to the hospital and reserved rooms for Chas and Henzie, so it looks like it will be just Anne and Luke here after tomorrow."

Sarah squeezed Anne's arm a little tighter and answered, "Okay, honey. We will just take Anne back into town with us when we go on Sunday, then." She nodded to Anne so that Anne wouldn't argue with her.

Anne finished her cookie dough as she stared out at the ocean which was now pitch black and ominous. She had to shake the depression that was enveloping her, so she got up with Sarah and ate some warm cookies just out of the oven. The three of them laughed at some YouTube videos that had come up on Jay's phone, and then Anne excused herself to go to bed.

As she slept, she dreamed of being carried in Rick's arms toward the sunset.

Chapter 29

When Anne woke the next morning, it was early and she decided to repeat what she had done the first day. She got her suit on, grabbed from fruit from the kitchen and descended the stairs to the beach. When she got to the sand, she chose to stay close to the stairs and just spread her towel out right there. She would sit in the morning sun for an hour then go get ready. She walked to the edge of the waves and let the freezing cold water touch her toes until they got used to the temperature. When she could stand it, she ventured further until the water covered her ankles when the waves came in. As she stood there and the waves massaged her feet, she looked down and saw a perfectly formed sand dollar about two feet away to her right. She bent down and picked it up.

All her life living near the beach, she had never found a perfect sand dollar. It was then that a thought occurred to her that this sand dollar represented Lila, and that she would soon be whole again. The feeling of peace surrounded her and she felt warm and tingly. She smiled into the sun and walked back to her towel.

She placed the sand dollar carefully at the top of her towel by her phone and sat down. She said a little prayer of thanks, and then began applying sunscreen to her legs. She remembered Rick rubbing sunscreen on her back only a few days ago, and tried to remember how that had felt.

What was wrong with him? She cannot be that dense. There has to be a reason for his sudden coldness. With the solitude and time to think, she tried to recall what had happened just before his behavior change.

She remembered that she noticed the change at dinner on the pier. So, something happened between lunch and dinner. During that time everyone had walked on the pier, then on the beach, and then on the boardwalk.

She had unfortunately walked with Will the whole time. Could he be jealous? He couldn't possibly think that she was interested in Will. Could he? Had he seen her hug Will by the shops? That probably looked cozier than it actually was. Was that it?

But then there was Rick's hug at the trailhead, and his smile as she messed with his hair by the ambulance. Then he was distant at the hospital. Was it because she sat next to Will? And then Will had carried her to and from the car when she was asleep. Was that it?

That has to be the reason. He must think I am

interested in Will. Good grief, doesn't he know me? How could I possibly be interested in that goofball?

Then she started to feel angry. How can he possibly have any right to feel jealousy after his behavior with Lila *right in front of me* for more than two weeks? She wanted to scream.

She lay back on the towel and tried to calm herself down. He was gone. Again. And she was once again helpless to do anything about it. Come on, Anne, you could get his number from Jay and text him and tell him that he is still a fool, but you still want him. You could do that. She argued with herself for the next 30 minutes and then got up and returned to the house.

She placed the sand dollar on the bathroom counter so it could completely dry out. She planned on preserving it and giving it to Lila when she got better. She took a shower and got herself ready for the day, still arguing with herself.

In the end she decided that she was going to enjoy her time at the beach house while she supported the Musgroves, and then she was going to go home, pass that stinking nursing test, and get on with her life. She no longer wanted to live with her family. She had spent these short few days away from them and marveled how much better she felt about herself. She even wondered if she could move out before she found a job. Certainly, she could prevail upon Jane Russell to let her stay with her for a month or two.

She had to move on.

Chapter 30

"Of course, you can stay with me." Jane laughed into the phone, "I thought you'd never ask."

Anne was in the backseat of Jay's BMW on her way home. They were about an hour out of Malibu sitting in traffic, with about another hour's drive to go.

"Can I come straight to your house in about an hour? I don't even want to go home," Anne asked. "I'll just go by when they are at the club and pack up my stuff, so I don't even have to talk to them."

"I can certainly help you with that," Jane answered slowly, "but you will have to speak with them at some point."

"I know. Just not today."

Anne said goodbye and ended the call. After a few minutes of silence, Sarah turned around in her seat to see Anne's face. It was beaming.

"Whoohooo!!!" Sarah yelled as she threw both fists in the air and Jay added his own yell of solidarity and support.

Anne had confided her plan to move in with Jane to the Harvilles the day before when they left the hospital after their last visit to Lila. She made Jay promise not to say anything to Rick. He had reluctantly agreed. Anne didn't share her theory about Rick's behavior with either of them. But they had their own speculations, and Anne neither confirmed nor denied them. She did not want any of this getting back to Rick in any form.

Lila had come out of the coma on the day they weaned her from the drugs. She was still slightly confused, but she knew who she was and who everyone else was, so her only memory loss was of the actual accident. She remembered the hike, but nothing after they got to the rock she was sitting on before she jumped. The doctors wanted to keep her in the hospital until the swelling in her brain was completely gone. They did an MRI every morning to check it. They predicted she would be there at least another week.

Anne and Sarah visited Lila every day until they left Sunday afternoon after Anne gave Lila the sand dollar. Luke was there with the family constantly and was often Lila's only visitor while the Musgroves rested or ate. Anne was sure that he had developed feelings for Lila, but didn't say anything. No one else seemed concerned that Luke hardly knew Lila, because Lila was enjoying his attention, and they seemed to be getting to know each other quickly. He hardly ever left her side and when he did, she asked where he was. Rick was forgotten.

Maybe Rick was right to leave when he did, so

that he could remove himself from Lila's company at an appropriate time. Anne could only speculate, and it was driving her crazy that her thoughts had been focused on this rampant speculation for the last four days. She had to shake it, and move on. He left, and she would probably not see him again.

Her test was in a week, and she needed to buckle down and review everything. She was counting on this distraction to get her mind off Rick.

When they finally pulled off the freeway in Eden Grove, Anne was antsy to get herself settled at Jane's. It was a new horizon. A new life that was free of Elizabeth and Walt Elliott. She could not completely divorce herself from them because she adored her nephews and the Musgroves, so she would have to endure Mary. But she now had a fresh perspective and a resolve to not let Mary walk all over her. She knew what she had to do. She wasn't fooling herself that it would be easy, but she knew she had to do it for her own sanity.

She hugged Sarah and Jay after they pulled up to Jane's house and were getting her things from the trunk of the car.

"Thank you for everything." Anne said as she hugged them. "We will keep in touch this time."

"Definitely," Sarah nodded. "You need to text me every day with an update. I want to know the play-by-play of your family drama so I can encourage and support."

Anne laughed, "Of course. You will love the drama."

"We only live an hour from here," Jay added, "We should meet for dinner to celebrate when you pass the boards."

"I don't want to wait that long," Anne said, "the results take, like, three months or so to post."

"Oh, then sooner." Sarah said excitedly, "How about after you *take* the tests?"

"Perfect," Anne said, "I'll let you know. Maybe next week?"

They both got back in the car and waved as they drove off.

Chapter 31

"And that is all of it."

Anne and Jane were sitting in Jane's living room, and Anne had just filled Jane in on everything that had happened in the last three weeks.

Jane could only nod. She patted Anne's knee and then wrapped her arms around her.

"Things are looking bright for you, my dear." Jane said as she held onto Anne.

Anne pulled away and nodded.

"I cleaned out the downstairs suite for you. The one with the separate entrance. Janice got married, so she doesn't live in anymore. And she only comes in on the weekdays. I just eat out on the weekends now."

Janice was Jane's live-in maid and cook. She was at least ten years older than Jane.

"She got *married*?" Anne was shocked. "Where did she meet this husband?"

"Online."

Anne laughed imagining this 70-year-old woman online dating. "I would love to see her profile page."

Jane grinned and agreed. "Her granddaughter helped her with it. It was pretty hip."

"When did this happen? And why didn't you tell me?"

"Last Christmas. And I thought I had told you. I must be forgetting things."

"Christmas was rough. I probably forgot."

"Well Christmas is always a tough time for your family. No worries."

They got up and went into the room where Anne would be staying. It was large, but not large enough to move a chair near one of the windows. The windows were on either side of the bed. Anne would have to completely rearrange the furniture to be able to have her window seat. She was instantly disappointed, but shook it off. She would have to deal with it. It wasn't for long, and then she would find her own place.

Jane hadn't had to clear much out. "I really haven't done much with this room since Janice left, so it was easy to get ready for you. You can change anything you want. We have the same taste. Just let me know, and we can go shopping. I've wanted to redo this room for years, so we can have fun with it."

Anne hugged her, "You are a great friend."

Anne started putting things away from her suitcase and other bags from the trips, and when she was done, she found Jane in the kitchen.

"Do you think you could text my dad to see where he is? I want to go get some things from my room, and get my car, but not if they are there."

Jane grabbed her phone and went to work. Anne got some juice from the fridge and sat at the island on a barstool. Jane's backyard was in full bloom. She was a bit of a green thumb and had her yard blooming with something all year round. The summer had been cool so far for Southern California, but the heat was inevitably coming. There were still spring blooms on the trees and Anne could smell gardenias.

"He is at the club for some golf tournament till late, let's go."

They headed over to Anne's house. Anne looked up the road to see if Mary was home. She didn't want to run into her either. She couldn't see any cars, so she was relieved. They were probably all at the club.

Anne looked through the house. It was exactly like she left it. Those two had not unpacked anything else since returning from the lake. A whole week. Well, it probably would never get done then, because Anne certainly wasn't going to do it. She laughed to herself.

She grabbed two empty boxes and filled them with things from her room and took them out to Jane's car. Jane was helping pack up her bathroom, which added only two additional boxes to the car. Anne grabbed most of her clothes out of her closet and put them in the back seat of her Camaro. She didn't have much so it was easy. She emptied her drawers and bookshelves into three more boxes.

When she had cleaned out her room she went downstairs and looked around. She found her mother's favorite Lladro figurine of a girl pushing a flower cart in the China cabinet that she had already unpacked, and then went through the boxes in the office and took some books that were special to her.

She stood in the entry with Jane for a minute trying to think of anything else she might be forgetting. When she couldn't think of anything she looked at Jane, nodded, and walked out to her car.

There were boxes of hers still in the garage, but she could come back for them. There was no room in either car at this point.

* * *

"That felt good,"

Anne and Jane were eating dinner after moving all Anne's things into her new room.

"Haha, yes." Anne looked at Jane with appreciation. "Thank you for making it possible."

"You know you are welcome to stay here as long as you like." Jane grabbed Anne's hand. "You are the daughter I never had, and I have wanted you to do this for years."

Anne's phone buzzed.

"It's Dad." Anne frowned. "He is asking when I am arriving. He probably needs me to do something."

"Like finish their unpacking?" Jane laughed.

"Probably…well, here goes."

Anne texted her father and let him know she was staying with Jane from now on, and wouldn't be home. She would come sometime the following week to get her things. There was a brief texting argument, and then he sent a frowny face emoji and let her alone.

Fifteen minutes later she got a scathing text from Elizabeth about how she was deserting the family in their hour of need.

"Dramatic." Anne whispered and showed Jane the text and Jane burst out laughing.

"*Hour of need*???...She is just upset that you are not there to do all the unpacking, cooking, cleaning, and *everything else*." Jane noted.

Anne typed for a minute and showed Jane her drafted response.

"You are just mad that now you have to do all the work around the house. Get a life, Eliza. I am no longer your servant."

Jane wrinkled her nose, then smiled.

"Too harsh?" Anne asked.

"She needs to hear it at some point." Jane nodded and pretended to hit a send button in the air.

Anne sent the text. Elizabeth never responded.

Chapter 32

Anne was feeling confident. She had just taken the nursing test. She felt really good about it. She had known most of the answers and was reasonably confident that she had gotten most of the ones where she had been unsure. She was a natural. Her courses in college had been easy and almost second nature. She had a natural affinity for nursing.

Now it was a waiting game. During this past week at Jane's, she had applied for positions at three local hospitals pending her test results. Her interviews had gone well, especially considering she had been out of school for 10 years. It helped that her schooling had been completed at a university famous for its nursing program, and her grades had been exceptional.

She was on her way back home when her phone buzzed. At a stoplight, she checked to see who it was. It was her dad.

Now what?

Anne waited until she was home before she opened the text. He wanted her to come home. He hadn't seen her since the lake house and he missed her and wanted her to come home. She knew there was no way he actually missed *her*. He just missed all the things she did for him.

She decided to compromise and sent him a text that said she would come over in the morning and pick up the rest of her things. They could talk then.

She had not told him about her nursing goals and decided that it was safe to tell him since she was no longer living there. Being away from him permanently made her bolder and more courageous. She could tell him how she felt and then leave. She didn't have to stay any longer than she wanted.

Jane was in the kitchen and Anne told her of her plan.

"Do you want me to go with you?"

"No." Anne smiled, "I think I can handle him. Eliza won't be there. It is Tuesday, so tomorrow morning is her tennis lesson at the club. She never misses. I think she likes her instructor."

Jane laughed and then added, "Because I will go with you if you need some moral support."

"I know, thank you."

Anne filled Jane in on her test and Jane was excited to hear that Anne had done well.

"Shall we celebrate?" Jane asked.

"Actually, I am meeting Sarah and Jay tonight," Anne said. "Tomorrow? After I talk to dad? We could meet for lunch at Graziella's."

"That sounds perfect."

Anne went to her room to get ready for her

dinner date with the Harvilles. It had been over a week since they had dropped her off at Jane's. Sarah had texted her everyday with encouragement and occasional updates on Lila. Luke had been keeping Jay apprised of Lila's progress. Her last text had been about Lila being scheduled for discharge this coming Friday.

It was amazing and remarkable that Luke was still there. Apparently, he had asked Jay if he could stay at the house until Lila was released, and Jay had let him.

When Anne was ready, she went to tell Jane she was leaving. She had decided to wear the same sundress that she had worn that first afternoon when they had all gone to the pier. Her hair was up in a high ponytail.

"Where are you meeting them," Jane looked up from her book.

"We decided on Glendale, because anywhere halfway between here and Santa Monica is not the safest of neighborhoods. Jay said there is a great Italian deli and bistro there that he used to go to as a kid. Tuesdays they have karaoke."

Jane burst out laughing.

"No, no, no." Anne had to laugh as well. "We are not going there for the karaoke. I don't have any idea why I said that."

Jane was still laughing as Anne left through the front door.

Chapter 33

Jay and Sarah were already there. Jay pulled out a chair for Anne to sit down, and Anne looked around the place. It was cute and crowded, which is always a good sign. You know the food is good if it is crowded.

"So…?" Sarah looked at Anne intently.

Anne looked dejected and said, "Well, it was really hard, and…I don't know…" Then she smiled, "just kidding. I think I nailed it."

"Then you probably have three jobs as soon as you get the results, right?" Jay put his hand up for a high-five.

"And nurses can have more than one job, right?" Sarah clapped her hands.

"Let's not get too excited," Anne laughed. "I only want one job at a time."

"No, I mean…I've heard that you can be on call at different facilities." Sarah looked confused, "Is that wrong?"

"I think you can be, but I want to start small and get a feel for the different departments." Anne picked up the menu, "I don't know what kind of nursing I will enjoy most. There are so many options, and specialties."

They looked over the menu and ordered an appetizer and drinks. While they waited, Jay filled them in on Lila.

"She will be released on Friday in the morning. The swelling is almost completely gone, and she has been up and walking the halls once or twice a day. They even let her walk outside today."

"Did she attempt some cheer jumps from the garden walls or benches in the atrium?" Anne asked with a straight face.

"Anne." Sarah tried to suppress a smile.

"Sorry, I couldn't resist."

"Come on, now," Jay tried to be serious.

Anne sat up a little, "You come on, Jay. I feel like I can say this now that she is going to be okay. Her behavior for those first two days was nuts. She was acting like a 12-year-old. I love her like a sister, but she was driving me crazy."

Jay nodded, "True. You are just saying what we were all thinking."

"Are you sure it wasn't because you were a little bit jealous?" Sarah said as she took a drink of her lemonade. Jay looked confused.

Anne grabbed her water and took a sip before replying. She decided to be honest, "No. I'm not sure about that. Maybe my jealousy made her behavior worse for me somehow."

"Jealousy? Who were you jealous of? Of Lila?"

Jay, clearly lost, looked from Sarah and Anne a few times, and when neither responded he shook his head and changed the subject to something he thought he understood, "Rick is a mess, by the way."

"Oh… that's too bad," Anne stuck her lower lip out in an exaggerated pouty face.

"Wow, Anne," Jay said wide-eyed, "you sure are a different person from when you first arrived at the beach house."

"That may be true," Sarah added as she looked at Jay, "but this…" she pointed at Anne, "…is the Anne I know from school."

Anne smiled.

Sarah continued, "I don't know how she was acting before I got to Malibu, but this Anne sitting here, is the Anne I knew 10 years ago."

"Why are you so different?" Jay asked.

Sarah must not have filled him in. That was surprising, but okay. Anne needed to own it, and what better way to do that than to explain it to someone in her own words.

She started with Rick's proposal and her refusal, and explained to Jay all about her family, from her mom, to her father and sisters and the hell she had allowed herself to be living in for the last 10 years. She wrapped it up with the Reader's Digest version of the two weeks at the lake.

Jay stared, aghast, through the entire monologue, and when she was done, he took a drink, and whispered, "You and Rick? …Rick *proposed* to you?"

Anne nodded.

"I had no idea. He has never said one thing about ever being almost engaged. When I met him, we were interns at the same firm, and he was an angry, focused guy with something to prove. I never knew why." He looked at Sarah with a furrowed brow, "And you never told me any of this."

Sarah shrugged, equally surprised, "I thought you knew…"

He took another drink and kept going. His mind was racing. It all made sense now.

"That was how he knew to move that chair for you…and why he avoided Will. I thought Will had said something to offend him early on—which was no stretch, believe me. But it was because of you. Will was going after you. And you were being polite and charming." It was almost like Jay was talking to himself.

Sarah and Anne exchanged amused looks as Jay stared glassy-eyed at the spinach dip that the girls were eating and continued talking.

"He was saying things that made no sense at the time, but now that I have context…" Jay looked slowly up at Anne, "I would bet my life that he is still in love with you."

He said that with such a serious expression that it gave Anne goosebumps and butterflies in her tummy.

"Well, he has a real interesting way of showing it." She said softly.

The server chose that exact moment to appear at the table to take their order. They scrambled with their menus and managed to figure out what they wanted quickly.

When the server left to put their order in, Jay continued, "I'm serious. It totally explains his behavior for this last week, and even the few days he was at the beach house. He has barely spoken to anyone, and has been short with his assistant, who even complained to my assistant yesterday. He is usually a pretty closed off person, but this week has been ridiculous. He won't even talk to me. We usually meet for lunch every day, but I haven't seen him since he left the beach house, and he knows I have been back for a week. He has answered the few messages I've sent him with only one or two words."

Sarah and Anne were wide eyed as Jay talked on in a giant run-on sentence. Sarah interrupted, "You haven't said anything to me about this."

Jay kept on like she hadn't said anything, "He's like my brother. I think I know him pretty well, and now this bomb is dropped on me that he was almost engaged...I mean, I thought I knew everything about him..." he trailed off and looked into space for a moment then continued, "I mean, I knew he didn't date much, but we never really talked about girls...we were just so focused on the work...getting our ideas and our vision coded and ready for the public."

He stopped suddenly and looked up sheepishly, "I'm sorry. Am I rambling?"

Both women laughed, and Sarah playfully bopped him upside the head, "just a little."

"I think a marriage proposal rejection is something that might stay in the vault for even the best of friends." Anne offered. "I really hurt him. I wouldn't hold it against him. It's probably a pride thing."

Sarah added, "Anne didn't tell anyone but me and her friend, Jane, till just now."

"Wow," is all Jay could say.

They were silent…lost in thought until their food arrived. Then Jay asked, "How do *you* feel, Anne?"

"About Rick?" She picked up her sandwich and looked at it thoughtfully as Jay nodded. "I have never stopped loving him." There. She said it again. Now three people knew.

"Well, crap…you need to tell him that."

"I told him ten years ago when he walked out. It was the last thing I said to him."

Jay was unsure how to respond to that.

"He has had ten years to…" Anne paused, "…to change his mind…to find me…I don't know. I wasn't going to beg. He made his choice. The male ego is a delicate thing."

"Then I need to tell him." Jay said resolutely.

"No." both women exclaimed together, and then pointed to each other laughing, "JINX."

Anne added something she hadn't before, "Rick knows that I had another marriage proposal since his, and I declined. And he knows I declined it because I wasn't in love the other guy."

"But if he thinks you are with Will, he is going to stay away." Jay argued.

"Ughh." Anne rolled her eyes. "Another male ego thing. Let's talk about something else please."

Jay and Sarah exchanged a look and then started talking about having Anne come back to the beach house in two weeks for the Fourth of July.

"There's a big city thing on the boardwalk all day, and then fireworks at night off the pier." Sarah said, "Malibu has to launch the fireworks over the water so the mountains don't catch fire."

"It's a thing." Jay added, nodding.

They finalized plans for the 4th, and settled that Anne would stay with them for the entire weekend. Then Anne asked Jay to tell her all about his software and his work. He managed to talk about Rick and his role in both of their success, because he couldn't avoid it. They had worked together from the start and were good partners. Anne was glad to finally hear Rick's story and was proud of him. No matter what he did, or how stupid he was acting, she still loved him and couldn't deny it anymore. And with the slight hint that he may still love her, she was feeling more hope in her future than she had in a long time.

They parted with the promise that Anne would meet them in Malibu on July 3rd.

As Anne drove off, Sarah turned to Jay, "We are inviting Rick for the 4th, too, right?"

"We certainly are."

"And not telling either of them…"

"Damn straight."

Chapter 34

"Hi Dad."

Walt looked his middle daughter up and down and then leaned in and gave her a kiss on the cheek. Walt wasn't a hugger.

"Hello, Anna-bella."

They walked into the house to the formal living room and sat across from each other. Walt sat on the sofa, and Anne sat in one of the wing chairs. Anne looked around and noticed that the boxes that had been there when she came to get her things were gone. Someone must have either unpacked them, or put them in the garage.

Walt didn't say anything at first so Anne decided to dive right in. She didn't want to be there long and chance running into Elizabeth. One at a time.

"Dad, I took the nursing boards yesterday and I am going to get a job as a nurse as soon as the results come back. I know I did well, so I'm not worried that I won't pass. But if I don't, I will just keep taking the test until I pass. I'm determined. You paid a lot of money for me to get my education and I am not going to let that investment be wasted."

She stopped to see if he was going to say anything and when he didn't speak right away, she kept going.

"I am going to get my own place as soon as I am working. Jane is very gracious to let me live with her until I can find a place."

Walt looked pained and annoyed at the same time.

"Anna…" Walt wrinkled his brow and pursed his lips, "Why can't you do all of that and still live here? I don't understand." He looked old all of a sudden.

"Well, Dad, that is a whole other thing." She sat forward in the chair so her body language would show resolve. "I cannot stay here anymore. You and Elizabeth expect me to run this household all alone. Neither of you lift a finger to help out. You both expect me to be Mom."

Walt looked like he had been stabbed, "But…Anne…" He was clearly surprised that she had mentioned her mother, and the defensive stance he had adopted started to crumble.

"No… wait until I'm done. I have to say all of it." Anne took a deep breath. "I have thought a lot about this, so let me get it out. For a long time, I have stayed here with no real purpose other than taking care of you and Eliza. Now, if doing that had been a pleasure and a joy, then we wouldn't be sitting here. But you and Eliza are ungrateful, demanding, entitled, and selfish. You only do what you want to do. And I do all the things you don't want to do. I cook and clean like Cinderella and have never been thanked or acknowledged. I feel like a slave or a servant, not like a daughter or a sister. This move was the last straw. I had to twist your arms to get you both to pack your office. I packed and unpacked everything else. We lived in a 6000 square foot house full of a lifetime of things that I packed *by myself*. I singlehandedly sorted through everything and decided what to give away and what to bring with us. If Jane hadn't come to help me for those few days, I would have been completely alone through the whole process."

Anne watched his expression vacillate between angry haughtiness, and sorrow. She forged on.

"You don't speak to me, and neither does Eliza. The entire ride to the lake—the three-hour drive— you said one thing to me. Do you remember what you asked me?"

Walt looked past her toward the window in the kitchen and nodded. "I asked you if you needed to stop at the rest area."

"Exactly. You chattered on with Elizabeth for three hours and never once included me in any of it. I have been ignored for the last 10 years, and I won't live like that anymore. That week in Malibu at the beach house, I started to realize that I have not been myself, and I didn't like who I had become. I was a shell of a person."

Walt looked down at his hands and surprised her for once. Without looking up at her he said, "I'm so sorry Anne. I didn't realize."

She wasn't expecting this and it disarmed her, "I'm sorry, too, Dad. I have been putting up with it without saying much, and that wasn't fair either. I should have said something a long time ago."

"No, my dear. It is my fault entirely." Walt stood up and walked over to their family picture that had been taken two years before Anne's mom passed. It was one of the only things Anne had put up on the wall when they moved. It had been taken at the Musgrove's lake house of all places. Walt and Grace sat on a bench under one of the big trees and the girls stood behind them. Anne and Elizabeth had both been in college and Mary was a senior in high school. They were all smiling and happy. It was Anne's favorite family photo.

He stared at the photo of his late wife. "I just miss her so much. All the things she did. All the things she was and I wasn't. She was my rock and my best friend. My life was easier when she was in it."

Anne got up and put her arm around him as they gazed at the photo. "Mom was the best."

Walt nodded and went back to the sofa. Anne followed him and sat next to him this time. "Dad, I'm going to be honest with you. You need to get it together and do something before you run out of money. There's not much money left from the sale of the house. Elizabeth needs a job, and so do you."

"I know." He turned to Anne and smiled. "I'm sorry, honey."

Anne put her arms around her father, which was something she had not done in a long time, and kissed his cheek. He didn't pull away, so she squeezed for a few moments and then let go.

"I love you, Dad, and thank you for listening and understanding."

Walt nodded and then admitted, "I will be honest with you. I already got an earful from June and Landry. They called me a few days ago and shook me up a bit. I did not take it well, and I will need to call them and apologize. I have had a lot of thinking time. June really got me when she told me that your mother was probably screaming at me from the grave because I have let our family fall apart. She was brutal."

Anne was once again surprised. "What else did they tell you?" She was a little worried that June had told him about her nursing plans after promising not to.

"That was about it," Walt ran his hands through his hair. "Why?"

She was relieved. "I just wondered if there was more."

"Well, I guess Landry mentioned that he had noticed Elizabeth and Mary didn't treat you very well. It made me think."

"Well, thank you for thinking about it, Dad, it means a lot." She got up to leave, "I need to grab a few things from the garage."

He watched her get up and walk to the door to the garage... and then got up with her.

"Can I help you?"

Anne was shocked, but hid it well, "Yes, Daddy, thank you."

They found the few boxes in the garage with her name on them and transferred them to her car.

"You know, Dad, we have all dealt with our grief in different ways," She turned to him as she opened her car door, "And it is time to move forward."

He kissed her forehead and then stood in the driveway and waved as she backed out and drove away.

She smiled and took a deep breath. One down. Now she had to figure out how she was going to deal with Elizabeth.

As she pulled into Jane's driveway, her phone buzzed.

It was a text from her dad telling her not to worry about Elizabeth. He would take care of explaining everything to her so that Anne didn't have to do that again. Talking to Elizabeth would be way more confrontational, so she was relieved and grateful. Now she need only worry when she would see Elizabeth again and how she would be treated. But since Anne was used to indifference or hostility from Elizabeth, anything apart from that would be a relief.

Anne was actually feeling very proud of her dad. Maybe things were going to change. This was certainly a step forward. It made her think that she should have done this years ago.

But, better now than never.

Chapter 35

The next two weeks were really fun. Jane insisted on redecorating Anne's room, so they spent the first week at the design center getting ideas and then the second week watching their ideas come to life while the contractors did their thing.

They chose a light blue paint for the walls, and then drapery and bedspread fabric that complimented each other. The draperies were a large floral print with mainly dark pink and yellow flowers, with dark green leaves in a dark blue field, and the bedspread was a two-inch blue and white stripe with the floral print as the pillow shams. They found a smaller bed frame in distressed white wood so that a chair would fit next to one of the windows and Anne picked out an overstuffed chair with dark pink colored fabric to which they added a dark green pillow with yellow polka dots.

Anne was worried that Jane was doing too much for her, but then realized that Jane was having more fun than she was. They walked arm in arm everywhere and laughed like a mother and daughter.

There were already shelves and a nightstand in the room that loosely matched the style of the new bed, so Jane just had them refinished in the distressed white style to match the bedframe. The only thing missing was an area rug. The flooring in the room was hardwood, and Jane wanted to soften it up with a big rug.

Everything was completed, except for the rug, two days before Anne was set to go to Malibu for the holiday weekend.

The room looked fantastic. As Anne was finishing up settling her things back in place Jane came in to see if she was hungry.

"Let's go to that new bakery on Grand Ave. and try a sandwich." Jane suggested with a smile, "it is a beautiful day, and I think I remember seeing a small outdoor seating area."

Anne put her last bit of clothing away in the dresser and threw her hands in the air, "Finito!" She then threw her arms around Jane, "Thank you for all of this. I feel like new person."

When they got to the bakery, it was moderately crowded, but they were able to grab one of the outdoor tables when they got their food. They ate in silence for a few minutes as they enjoyed what was turning out to be some great food.

"This is really good," Anne said between bites, "I wonder if their pastries are this good, as well."

"We will get some to go and try them later at home," Jane said after finishing her bite. Then Jane stared across the street. "When did that store open?"

Anne looked in the direction of Jane's gaze and saw a carpet and rug store she had never seen before. "I know where we are going after we finish eating," Anne giggled, as Jane pointed at her with a grin.

"You know it, sister."

They finished their meal and then went back into the bakery and chose some pastries that looked delectable for later, and then walked across the street to the new store.

The store was full of beautiful Persian and Chinese rugs, and had some more modern choices toward the rear of the store. Anne and Jane were contemplating two long-looped shag rugs when suddenly Mary was standing in front of them.

"Well, if it isn't my long-lost sister," Mary exclaimed with her hands on her hips.

Anne looked up startled and tried to decide if Mary was being sarcastic or genuine. Normally when someone says something like that, they follow it up with a hug or a hearty handshake. But Mary just stood there. She was smiling, but there was no hug forthcoming. Anne decided to be the bigger person. She grabbed Mary in a big hug.

Mary hugged her back after a slight hesitation.

"Hi, Mary," Anne smiled as she let go of her sister, "How have you been? How are the boys? How is Wally's arm?" It was then that Anne noticed that Elizabeth was standing just a little behind Mary. Anne kept her focus on Mary for the moment.

"I am fine. Wally gets his cast off in about a week..." Mary fell into her usual rant about all things Mary, apparently forgetting that Elizabeth was standing behind her. "...and Charlie said we should get a new rug once we finished the tile, so here we are."

Anne nodded, "Jane is looking for a new rug for her home, as well." Anne nodded toward Jane, and Mary gave Jane a hug. While they hugged, Anne acknowledged Elizabeth tentatively.

"Hello, Eliza."

Elizabeth looked like she was experiencing an inner war. She didn't move, but nodded to Anne.

Anne decided to focus on Mary. Why give Elizabeth attention for being a pill? Mary was being more than polite, and that should be rewarded, not Elizabeth's cold behavior.

Elizabeth stood back in an attitude of aloof disinterest while the other women discussed rug options, and Mary added her "expert" designer opinion to the rugs that Jane was considering, and with a nod from Anne, Jane chose the cream, long-looped shag rug that had little blue flecks in it.

While Jane was purchasing the rug and arranging for it to be delivered later that day, Elizabeth finally approached Anne and Mary, "Anne, Dad told me what you were doing and explained why." She paused as if wondering how to say what she said next, "but I don't get it. It feels like you are deserting us. Why are you breaking up the family?"

Mary turned to Anne with an expression on her face as if she had the exact same question and wanted to hear the answer.

Anne decided to use a logical approach, "Eliza, do you even like me?"

Eliza was taken aback, "Why…of course I do, you are my sister."

Mary looked offended as well, "What the heck, Anne?"

"It really is a fair question, actually, for both of you." Anne took a breath. "Neither of you talk to me, ever. I don't think I have had a meaningful conversation with either of you for years. You only speak to me when you want me to do something for you."

Both sisters looked at each other and then back at Anne.

Anne continued, "I am going to ask you some questions that you don't have to answer. Just think about them. First question: I know that I am a lot like Mom, and you both are more like Dad, but did you both expect me to do all the things that mom did for you for the rest of your lives? I feel like you expect me to be Mom for you. Second question: six months after Mom died and I came home from school, I know we were all grieving, but neither of you bothered to ask me how I was doing. Did either of you care? I felt like I mourned for my mom all alone. I mean, we are sisters, for crying out loud. We are supposed to support each other and at least talk to one another. I would try to talk to you and you would shut me down. You never had time. So many things were more important to you, than I was."

Elizabeth was looking Anne right in the eye with a blank expression, but Mary was looking down.

"I'm not saying we have to be best friends, but we could at least be thoughtful and supportive of each other. I can't be the only one who cares about this anymore. It is a two-way street. We all loved our mother. What would she tell us to do right now? What would she think about all of this?"

Anne waited for a response, but not for very long. She didn't want to make things more awkward. She had said her peace, and now she could move on. Whatever happened next was up to them.

She walked past them toward the front of the store where Jane was waiting, then turned and gave them one last look and smiled, "I love you both. You need to stop acting like the only ones on this planet."

Jane put her arm around Anne and they left the store.

Chapter 36

"I heard everything you said, and I think it was everything they needed to hear," Jane said as they drove home.

Anne shook her head, "I just hope they listened, and they will think about it." Then she turned toward Jane, "But it is okay if they don't. I am not going to expect anything."

Anne's phone buzzed and she took it out of her purse to see that Sarah had texted.

"Just checking on your plans? What time are you planning on getting here?"

Anne answered that she would leave on the 3rd at 9:00 in the morning, so, allowing for traffic, she should get there by 11:30.

"Can't wait to see you!!" was Sarah's reply along with about 15 smiling emojis and hearts.

***

Sarah looked up from her phone. "She is leaving at nine, so she should get here by 11:30."

Jay looked up from his phone, "Well, Rick is *getting* here around nine. He won't have to deal with as much traffic as she will. He says he's leaving at eight."

"Hopefully she doesn't turn around when she pulls up beside his car in the driveway."

Jay looked alarmed, "Do you think she would do that?"

"I'm not altogether sure," Sarah answered. "I think her first reaction will be wondering if we said anything to him about our conversation at dinner."

"How can we let her know that we didn't?"

"I don't think we can without giving it away. We will just have to trust that she trusts us."

"And she will know we didn't tell him as soon as she walks in and sees his reaction to her being here."

Sarah laughed. "I can't wait to see his face. Anne will at least have a little warning."

"And hopefully this doesn't blow up in our faces." Jay grabbed his wife in a tight hug.

"If it does," Sarah whispered into his ear, "You will have an awkward time at the office for a while."

"I like Anne, and if Rick does something to blow it with her again, I will be the one causing the awkward all over him at work."

Chapter 37

"You've got to be kidding me?" Anne had her phone to her ear and was staring at Jane.

Jane looked concerned. Anne was talking to Mary. So, it could be any number of things from serious to trivial. But Anne's reaction was leaning toward the serious.

"That is just way too soon, don't you…?" Anne was obviously interrupted. Jane could hear Mary's voice, but not exactly what she was saying, but it sounded like the typical dramatic narrative Mary was famous for.

Anne had been just about to leave for Malibu when Mary called.

"Okay, calm down, Mary. They are obviously…"

Mary's voice again, even louder. Jane heard the word "accident" and the word "ridiculous."

"Okay, Mary," Anne was smiling now, rolling her eyes, shaking her head slightly, and giving off an infinitely less serious vibe.

Jane relaxed.

"Thank you for telling me, Mary. I will look forward to hearing about the wedding plans." Anne said after Mary stopped talking.

Jane perked up again, surprised, as Anne ended the call.

"Wedding plans? …What? …Who?"

"Okay," Anne laughed out loud, "So remember when I told you that when Lila Musgrove was in the hospital after her accident, that guy, Luke was ever present?"

Jane nodded.

"Well, evidently, he has not left her side for even a moment since the accident, and they are now engaged."

"Wait a minute," Jane did some math in her head, "That was only four weeks ago."

"Just about, yes."

"Good gravy."

"He must have been attracted to her before she jumped off the rock, and was drawn even closer when he was presented with the opportunity to be with her constantly. I have to admit, I thought he was a nice guy, but I didn't get to know him very well. He was really quiet."

"How has he been with her constantly? Does he work? Are the Musgroves here in town, or at the lake?" Jane asked in rapid fire.

"Uhh…" Anne tried to answer, "I think he works for Jay Harville, so I'll have to ask Jay when I get to Malibu about Luke's job status…and Mary said the family is all at the lake, so Luke is apparently with them there."

Jane asked the question that even Anne was wondering, "What did the family say about Rick? I mean, he as much as disappeared after the accident after being on Lila's leash for over two weeks."

"Well, I obviously didn't ask, but Mary did mention that Sophia told them that Rick called Henzie to check on Lila a few times in the first two weeks after the accident, but Lila never spoke to him for whatever reason, so he only actually spoke to Henz. Henzie made it clear to Rick that Lila was seeing someone else, but didn't say who."

"What a tangle." Jane rolled her eyes.

"I could tell that Rick was getting weary of Lila when we got to Malibu," Anne remembered, "So I don't think he is heartbroken. If anything, I think he is probably relieved."

Jane nodded. "Is Luke closer to Lila's age?"

"I think so."

"Well, this is exciting." Jane clapped her hands. "A wedding to look forward to…and a Musgrove wedding at that. It should be the event of the year."

Anne gave Jane a farewell hug and Jane said, "You know that you could just tell Rick that you still love him."

"Yeah, I could." Anne held onto Jane for extra comfort, "but I don't think I could take the rejection a second time."

"It might not go in that direction."

"Sarah and Jay would agree with you."

Jane pulled away startled, "Jay and Sarah know about you and Rick?"

"Yep," Anne said matter-of-factly as she

grabbed the handle of her rolling overnight bag, hefted her purse onto her shoulder and walked out the door, "Bye, Jane, I'll see you in a few days. Happy 4th!"

Jane stared after Anne and furrowed her brow in thought. Then she smiled, and thought, Anne is pretty smart, she has to know that those two have invited Rick to this weekend party. Right?

She's not stupid.

Chapter 38

I am so stupid, Anne thought to herself.

She texted Sarah after pulling up next to Rick's BMW. "YOU HAVE GOT TO BE KIDDING ME!" She sat in her car staring straight ahead. Was she this stupid? How had she not seen this coming? She rested her head on the steering wheel repeating, "stupid, stupid, stupid..." Her heart was beating hard, and she had a sudden nervous feeling in the pit of her stomach. She couldn't do this. She put the car in reverse and started to back up when her phone buzzed.

"Please come in the house," Sarah texted back. And then another "please" buzzed a moment later.

Anne's thoughts raced. Think, think. Did he know she was coming or not? It was logical to assume that he wouldn't be here if he knew she was coming, too. Especially after his abrupt exit almost a month ago. After all, as far as she knew, he still thought she was seeing Will.

That means that I know he is here, but he doesn't know I am coming, she thought. Did Sarah plan it this way?

OR, they told him she was coming and he came, knowing she would be here, too. That was encouraging if it were true.

***

Sarah looked at her phone then looked up at Jay and nodded her head toward the front of the house when Rick wasn't looking. Jay and Rick were talking about something work related. Jay smiled back at her and winked.

Rick noticed the wink, "I'm sorry, do you two want to be alone?" He laughed, "I didn't think I would be in the way here. You invited me, remember?"

"Oh, for heck sake," Sarah waved her hand at him, "You are not in the way. He just likes to wink at me." She gave Jay an exasperated look when Rick looked away. Jay laughed.

She was worried that Anne had not come in yet, but she couldn't get up and go see if she was still outside without giving it away.

***

Anne grabbed a cup of courage and decided that this weekend could be either the bitter end or a new beginning with Rick. She had to try, or she would never know. But she would definitely know for sure one way or another in the next few days. She was going to decide what her life was going to look like from now on, no matter what anyone else thought.

She got her bag from the trunk and strode confidently to the front door. She stopped, took a deep breath, then rang the bell and walked in.

Chapter 39

"ANNE!" Sarah said excitedly and jumped up as Anne walked into the great room. She also took care to watch Rick's reaction, which wasn't as exciting as she had envisioned. He just raised his eyebrows. As she ran across the room to where Anne was, she barely heard him ask Jay, "Oh, hey...Great. Is Will coming, too?"

Jay answered a little louder, "Why would Will be coming?"

Sarah threw her arms around Anne and whispered, "If we had told you, would you have come?"

Anne hugged Sarah a little too hard on purpose and replied softly, "Heck, no. I almost left just now, you dork."

Sarah stepped back and looked at Anne, "But you didn't."

"No. I didn't." Anne took another obvious deep breath. The nervous feeling was still there.

The girls walked over to the sofa where the guys were still sitting. Anne wanted to wipe that crazy smile off of Jay's face, but it was so endearing and hopeful that she let it go and smiled right back. Jay jumped up and welcomed her with a hug.

"Hello Anne," Rick smiled uncomfortably and got up and gave her a short, polite hug after Jay's.

"Hi Rick. How have you been?" Anne asked politely, wondering why he seemed more uncomfortable than she was. "I didn't know you would be here." Her heart was beating faster than normal, but she felt calm. She was aware that Jay and Sarah were watching them intently but silently. Rick seemed unaware of their scrutiny. He was just blatantly uncomfortable.

"Really?" he threw Jay an angry, questioning expression, then looked back at Anne, "I've been okay, considering." Rick answered simply. Short answers, just like Jay said. No friendly elaboration. No questions for her.

"That is good," She replied, unsure what to say next.

After a beat or two, Sarah suggested they go down to the beach with the sandwiches they had ordered and have a picnic of sorts.

Anne decided to just go with it. "That sounds great; I need some sun on this white body. Do you want me in the same room as before?"

"Unless you want an ocean view this time?" Sarah pointed to the wing where Anne had stayed before and told her to pick whichever room she wanted.

Anne grabbed her things and headed toward that

hallway and decided that an ocean view would be divine this time, so she chose the one with the bigger window and began unpacking her things.

After about ten minutes Sarah showed up in her bathing suit. A red, white, and blue retro 50s style bikini with high waist bottoms. Anne had put on the same blue and white polka dot suit she had worn that first day a month ago.

"So has he said anything?" Anne was putting her hair in a pony.

"I heard him ask Jay if Will was coming." Sarah smiled, "That was it."

"And Jay said?"

"Jay asked him why he thought Will would be coming, and Rick didn't reply."

Anne put her hands on her hips and rolled her eyes dramatically. "So, he thinks I'm seeing Will?"

"Yep, just like we thought."

"Hilarious."

Chapter 40

When Sarah and Anne got down to the beach the guys were already there. Anne made Sarah promise not to leave Rick alone with her just yet. She wasn't sure why, just that she was feeling the need for support and safety in numbers. She wasn't ready for the possibility of being ignored and rejected so soon after arriving.

Rick and Jay were playing Frisbee and Jay had the intercom on with Sarah's 80s music playlist. Rock Lobster was blaring. The perks of a private beach. Jay whistled at Sarah as the girls walked through them to sit closer to the water. Sarah's reaction to this macho move was to start walking like an over-the-top runway model to the beat of the music. Anne burst out laughing and joined in.

It was nice to just sit on the beach and listen to Jay and Rick talk while they tossed the Frisbee. They were working out new game ideas for Rick's company. She could listen to Rick's voice all day.

After about 15 minutes, the boys came to sit by the girls. Jay had grabbed the cooler that was by the stairs and handed out the sandwiches and chips he had ordered earlier and they all ate lunch there on the sand. The conversation was a little strained because of the elephant, but otherwise pleasant. Rick would steal glances at Anne that he probably didn't think she noticed, and she did the same. They talked about the city celebration at the pier the next day and what their plan was going to be. Jay and Sarah were extra talkative and filled in the awkward silences that happened every now and then. Anyone observing would assume the four were the best of friends and there were no problems.

After they finished eating, the guys went back to Frisbee and the girls continued to sunbathe after getting their feet wet in the surf for a few minutes.

Anne eventually turned over to lie on her stomach and had Sarah put sunscreen on her back, and then she must have dozed off. She had a hat over her face, so her face was protected. She knew she had fallen asleep because all of a sudden, an Eagles song turned into Howard Jones.

She raised her head slowly and noticed that Sarah and Jay were now playing Frisbee and Rick was sitting next to her looking out at the water. He was dripping wet, so she gathered he had just come from the water.

As she sat up, Rick offered to get her a drink, and she nodded. He came back from the cooler with a soda that she thanked him for, and took a few sips.

"How is the water?" Anne asked, "Is it terribly cold?"

Rick nodded, "It's cold, but you get used to it. It isn't rough and there's no rip tide." He turned to face her, "do you want to go in with me? It will cool you off."

She had to admit she was hot because the wind had died down a little from earlier.

"But you just went in," She reached over and messed with his wet hair. She was being really brave.

"I'll go in again with you," he stood up and held out his hand to help her up.

She grabbed his hand and stood up and then let go awkwardly, and started for the water. Holding his hand had been electrifying and she wished she could have held on. She may not like water sports, but jumping over and diving under waves was fun as long as she could touch and the water was not icy.

She stopped at the edge and let a wave lap over her feet. "EEEEE. It's freezing." She turned toward Rick and took a step like she was changing her mind and returning to her towel.

"Oh no," he blocked her way playfully, "Come on, Anne. You'll get used to it."

She felt her heart skip when he said her name, and he was looking at her with an expression she hadn't seen in a while. She hoped he couldn't tell that she was blushing.

They stood in silence where the water met the sand for as long as it took for her legs to become numb to the cold and she was able to venture farther out until she was almost waist deep when a wave would roll in.

It was pretty shallow for a few yards, so they stood in the perfect place to jump the shorter waves and dive under the bigger ones. After her first dive under, she came up really close to where Rick popped up and it startled her. He grabbed her arms to steady her since he could touch and she couldn't until the wave passed.

"Okay?" Rick let go of her when she could touch.

"Yeah, thanks." She grinned at him and then had to quickly dive under another wave.

After a few bigger waves that they had to dive under, the waves got smaller for a while so Anne didn't have to dive under them.

Rick took this opportunity to start a conversation. "So…how is Will?"

Anne almost burst out laughing, but was able to keep her composure and answer, "Why would you ask me about Will?" as she jumped over a wave. She had already decided that, if he asked, she was going to skirt around this subject just to torture him. The fact that he thought she would have been attracted to the most shallow, self-centered person she had ever met, annoyed her and she wasn't going to let Rick get away with that.

He looked confused; "Um…I thought that…well…" he stammered on like he'd forgotten how to speak English.

She jumped the next wave and said, "You thought what?" She had to concentrate hard to keep from smiling.

He waited until the next wave went by then said so softly that she almost didn't hear him, "Aren't you and Will dating?"

"What?"

"Look, Anne," He was dead serious and annoyed. She almost regretted what she was doing. "Are you dating Will?"

"Are you serious?" She shot him the most incredulous look she could muster and almost got hit by the next wave. The waves were getting bigger.

"Yes." He said after the wave went by.

The waves were big again and Anne didn't feel like diving anymore so she began swimming to shore and caught the next wave to body surf it. It took her most of the way in. She could hear Rick calling after her, and when she stood up and turned around, she watched him catch the next wave in.

Before he caught up to her, she turned and walked the rest of the way out of the water and back to her towel. She picked her towel up and shook the sand off so she could dry herself a little, and then spread the towel back on the sand and sat down.

She looked up to see Rick standing over her. He looked like he was expecting her to say something.

"I'd like to know why you think I am dating Will." Anne was going to make him explain this to her. Maybe it would sound crazy to him, too, if he said it out loud.

He sat down on his towel. Then looked out at the water as he said, "He was paying you a lot of attention when we were last here."

"Yes, he was. For a day and a half," She agreed. "Go on…"

"You looked very cozy when you were walking

on the boardwalk. I saw you hug him…"

"Yes, I hugged him." Anne agreed again, "Anything else?"

"Well…when he carried you into the house from the car after you fell asleep at the hospital…he kissed you."

Crap. Really?

It was Anne's turn to feel uncomfortable. Her eyebrows rose before she could stop them. No one had told her that. No wonder…

"I was asleep," Anne said defensively, "I had no idea he did that."

Rick looked at her, "I assumed that because he kissed you, you both had an understanding."

"Well, there was never an understanding that I understood," Anne decided to stop torturing him, "Will was cute, but he was self-absorbed, vain, and a player…." She paused for effect and looked right at Rick with a straight face, "…profoundly unattractive."

Rick's expression changed from cloudy brooding to pleasant relief with every word she said.

"When I hugged him on the boardwalk, it was because I had just told him that I wasn't interested in being his fling for the week, and he thought a hug was appropriate at that weird moment."

"Oh my gosh," He shook his head in unbelief, "I feel like an idiot…I've assumed all the wrong things."

He still wasn't off the hook. So, if he was feeling a little more comfortable at this moment, she was about to throw him back into the lion's den.

"Yes, you have…So, now… about Lila…how is

Lila?" She asked even though she knew all about Lila. She had cleared everything up for him. Now he needed to do the same for her.

His cloudy expression returned, and he looked out at the ocean, his mouth pressed in a thin line.

Jay chose that moment to announce over the intercom that they both were needed upstairs to decide what to order for dinner. Anne hadn't even noticed that Sarah and Jay had left them alone on the beach. Dang you, Sarah.

Anne quickly got up, shook out her towel and gathered her things and marched to the stairs. Rick didn't move. She looked back to see if he was following her, and he was still sitting on his towel staring at the ocean.

Chapter 41

"You weren't supposed to leave me," Anne said to the Harvilles as she walked into the kitchen. She shot Sarah an over-exaggerated scowl.

"Everything okay?" Jay asked, "Where is Rick?"

"He hadn't moved from his towel when I started up the stairs, so I don't know." Anne took a seat on one of the barstools facing away from the ocean view window. Jay and Sarah were standing on the other side of the island facing the big window, "I just cleared up the Will situation for him, and had just asked him about the Lila situation when you announced that you needed us up here. I didn't give him a chance to answer before I left. Did either of you tell Rick about what we talked about at dinner two weeks ago?"

"Nope," Sarah said as Jay shook his head. They were speaking softly in case Rick walked in.

"So, he hasn't been told anything about how Lila is doing, or what I have been doing?"

Jay answered, "I have barely spoken to him in the last month, like I said at dinner. I was almost surprised he showed up this morning."

"My sister, Mary, told me that he has called Henzie a few times to check on Lila, but hasn't spoken to Lila."

"Speaking of Lila," Jay looked thoughtful, "I haven't heard from Luke in about a week, how is she doing?"

Before Anne could answer, Sarah gave her an intense look, then looked past Anne's head at something behind her.

"Yes," Rick's voice came from behind Anne, "How is Lila?"

He took a seat on the barstool one away from Anne and turned to give Anne his full attention for her answer. Anne realized at that moment that she was about to drop a bomb on all of them. If Jay hadn't spoken to Luke in a week...

"Lila is doing great, according to Mary," Anne had been looking at Jay, but then turned to look at Rick as she said; "She just got engaged."

"What!!??" Sarah slammed her hands down on the bar. Rick and Jay were silent and staring right at Anne. Sarah continued, "Who could have possibly? ...was there an old boyfriend?"

Anne let it sink in for a full minute to see if they could figure it out for themselves.

"Luke?" Jay asked quietly.

Anne nodded and watched Rick's expression changed from relief, to confused and thoughtful, and back again as he stared at the countertop.

"I was wondering how Luke knew so much

about her recovery," Jay said as Sarah put her arm around him.

"Apparently he has been staying with the family at the lake house while she recovers." Anne further explained. "He has never left her side."

Jay ran his hand through his hair and shook his head. "I'm going to go shower." He unfolded himself from Sarah's embrace and walked quickly to the stairs. Sarah looked at both Rick and Anne and followed her husband.

Anne got up and mumbled something about going to clean up, and once again left Rick sitting and staring straight ahead.

Chapter 42

Anne was the first one to emerge from her room all cleaned up. She had chosen wide-legged khaki capris and a blue and white striped short-sleeved denim button down. She had blown her hair out and curled it and put on a little make up.

She grabbed an apple from the island and sat down in "her" chair in front of the window to watch the water and wait for the others. She was delighted that Sarah had kept the chairs here in front of the window.

She was worried about Jay. His sister had only been gone a year, and Luke was already engaged to another girl. It had to be a blow.

She could hear Jay and Sarah coming up the stairs, "…I know, honey, but you *did* want him to snap out of it and not be so depressed." Sarah was saying.

"I wanted him to start living again, not jump right into another relationship."

They appeared at the top of the stairs, and noticed Anne sitting there.

Anne agreed, "It think it is a little fast myself… and Luke is not the first person I would have thought would have been attractive to Lila…"

"But maybe they are each what the other needs." Sarah said philosophically.

Rick was following close behind them and added, "Fast doesn't even come close to how we should describe this…It's like getting engaged at a speed dating event." Rick seemed to have gotten his voice back in the last hour, and his sense of humor.

Anne nodded in agreement and tried to smile at him, but he wasn't looking at her. He was making a beeline for the menus on the counter.

"I'm starving."

Sarah went over to the counter with Rick and they looked through the menus so they could make a choice.

Jay sat in the chair next to Anne, "I'm just blown away. How could he do this? How could he forget my sister so easily?"

Anne put her hand on his arm, "I know."

"She would not have done this to him so soon. She adored him. There was no other man for her."

"I know." Anne sat up straighter and tried to be supportive, "Once a woman finds her true love, no other man ever comes close."

"I thought it was the same for men. Luke even told me of his fierce love for Cassie even after she died, and that he would never love again." Jay shook his head, "A strong love like that is obviously not an enduring one, like you describe."

"He deserves to be able to find love again, and it may seem quick, but maybe Sarah is right. They have found something in each other that they need." Anne was so intent on helping Jay work through this shock, she was unaware that Rick and Sarah could hear everything they were saying and had stopped looking at the menus. Sarah watched Rick out of the corner of her eye as they both listened intently. She wondered if Anne was conscious of the fact that she was describing her own feelings in her efforts to comfort Jay.

"But the kind of love my sister shared with Luke…" Jay stared out the window, "How could he just forget that?"

"I agree with you," Anne turned to face Jay, "Maybe a man's love is strong, but a woman's love is strong *and* enduring. It remains strong even after all hope is gone."

"So, you are saying that our love is the strongest, but your love lasts the longest?"

Anne nodded.

"Well, this is certainly the case in this situation."

"And we can only wish the best for Luke and Lila."

Jay turned to meet Anne's gaze and smiled. "Thanks for your insight, and for helping me talk it out. It will just take some time to get used to."

Jay turned around to look at Sarah and Rick in the kitchen, and Anne followed his gaze. Both seemed frozen. Rick was staring at the counter, and Sarah was staring at Rick. Anne was suddenly self-conscious that he had heard everything she said. She couldn't be sure until Sarah looked her way and winked.

Her heart started beating. She realized what the things she had just said to Jay must have sounded like to Rick. She hoped against all hope he had actually heard her. *Yes, my dear, my love for you has endured even when there was no hope left.*

Sarah interrupted the silence in the room, "How about fajitas? I feel like Angelo's fresh guacamole, and their delivery is usually fast."

Jay jumped up as Rick and Anne nodded, and joined Sarah in the kitchen and began dialing the number on his phone. Rick went and sat on the sofa and took out his phone, and Anne turned back to look out at the ocean. As she looked straight out to the south, the sun was at about 2 o'clock in the western sky. Summer in SoCal meant the sun didn't start setting until 8:30, so even though it was at least 6 o'clock, the sun was still somewhat intense and unusually high in the sky. The water was starting to glitter, though. This was her favorite time of day.

After about ten minutes Rick got up and walked past Anne to the stairs. When he got to the top of the stairs, and only she could see him, he turned back and got her attention. He was holding his phone. He looked down at his phone, looked back at her and then pressed the phone with his thumb as if he just sent something, or ended a call. He gave Anne a rather intense look, pointed at his phone, then pointed at her, and then turned and went down the stairs.

What was all that? Did he just send her something?

She got up and went to her room where she had

left her phone and picked it up. There was a text from Rick.

Her heart started beating fast. She caught her breath and stumbled backwards as she tried to find somewhere to sit without taking her eyes off of the phone. As she found a place on the chair near the bed, she opened the message:

"I can listen no longer in silence. I must tell you how I feel. You pierce my soul. I have been half agony, half hope since you arrived this morning. Please tell me that I am not too late. Please say you still love me. I offer myself to you again with a heart that is even more your own than when you almost broke it 10 years ago. Don't say that a man's heart is less constant than a woman's. I have only ever loved you. I have been prideful, resentful, and stupid, but never inconstant. I have only been unsure of where your heart is. Forgive me.

I am going down to the beach. I will wait for you. If you still love me, my arms are waiting to hold you forever."

Anne read the message three times without breathing, then became conscious that she needed to breath. Tears began to roll down her cheeks. She dropped her phone, got up, and went to her huge window to see if she could see him. But she could not see any part of the beach and she remembered how the house hung over the beach so that you could only see water. She made her way as quickly as she could out to the family room and to the stairs that led to the beach.

Sarah and Jay were sitting on the sofa as she passed by and Sarah said something that she didn't hear and didn't acknowledge. Sarah and Jay exchanged a look of confusion and Sarah almost got up to follow her, but Jay stopped her, "Rick is down there…"

Anne was shaking as she tried to make it down the spiral stairs without falling. She stopped at the bottom where she was able to look up and see where Rick was.

He was standing near the water with his hands in his pockets looking out at the horizon.

She started walking toward him with her hands up to her face attempting to wipe her tears, "Rick?"

He turned at her voice and the look on his face said everything. He met her halfway and enfolded her in a desperate embrace. She began sobbing as she held onto him with all her strength. He buried his face in her neck, "I'm so sorry…so sorry…so sorry," he mumbled over and over in her ear.

"I've never stopped loving you," She whispered in his ear as she drew her head back and their lips met softly and tenderly, and then the kiss became more intense. She reached up and held his face with both hands as he slowly lifted her off the ground so her face was even with his.

Their kiss was filled with the pent-up longing from 10 years of being apart, and seemed to last forever until they finally pulled away to look in each other's eyes. Rick set her down and with his hands tangled in her hair began kissing her tears away, softly saying in between kisses, "I…love you…so much…never stopped…so happy...been…wanting…this…for so...long…"

Anne could not help but laugh during this tender display. She could not stop smiling. She pushed his face away to look at him again, "Me too." This look in his eyes was all she had ever needed and wanted. He leaned down and his lips barely touched hers and they shared another kiss even more exquisite than the first.

They held each other as they looked out at the ocean for what seemed like a long time until the intercom started playing music which snapped them back into reality.

"I'm still starving," Rick said out loud, still holding onto her tightly, "But this time, for food,"

Anne giggled, "I agree. I think it is time for dinner."

Sarah's voice interrupted the music, "We went looking for you and discovered you hugging on the beach. We waited as long as we could, but now the food is getting cold. Get up here, you two."

Hand in hand, they walked back to the stairs and began ascending the three flights to the main level. Halfway up Rick asked, "So how much do Jay and Sarah know about us?"

"Everything."

She had been climbing in front of him and he grabbed her waist and turned her around with a look of surprise, "Wait a minute, this whole time, they knew everything?"

"Sarah has known all along… you know that," Anne leaned toward him and gave him a quick kiss on his forehead, "but we told Jay two weeks ago when we met for dinner."

"You told Jay what, exactly?"

"That you proposed to me in college, I said no, but I was still in love with you." Anne said coyly and then added, "And he was not pleased that you had never told him about us."

"Oh wow. He's going to expect an explanation."

"Actually, I think we will all require an explanation of your behavior at the lake and then here before Lila's accident."

"Fair enough." He turned her back around and started to playfully push her up the stairs and then pulled her back into him and wrapped his arms around her and started nuzzling her neck, "I will tell you whatever you want to know. I was an idiot, and I will admit to anything as long as you love me."

"Deal," She giggled. She didn't think she would ever stop smiling.

They finished climbing the stairs and entered the kitchen hand in hand, to clapping and cheers from Sarah and Jay.

"Finally!" both Harvilles said at the same time and gave each other a high-five, and Jay added, "Get over here and eat. This is the best guacamole on the planet."

"Finally… we are here to eat? …or finally…?" Anne said as she held up Rick's hand in hers.

Sarah ran around the island and threw her arms around Anne while Jay yelled, "Both, of course!!"

Jay shook Rick's hand and they all dug into the best guacamole on the planet.

Chapter 43

"Dude, I wasn't going to tell you the long and sad story of my proposal rejection. It was just too embarrassing."

"But I thought we were best friends?" Jay pouted with exaggeration and then added seriously, "It would have explained so much of your behavior for the last 10 years…. I could have helped you." He and Sarah were sitting on one of the sofas holding hands, and Rick and Anne were on the other. Anne was sitting next to Rick with her legs underneath her. They were intertwined octopus style. They couldn't stop touching each other.

"Helped me with what?"

"Your stupidity."

"Of course."

Sarah chimed in with the question of the evening. "So now, tell us all about how you came to be in Eden Grove in the first place, and then explain the whole thing with Lila."

Anne nodded, "Yes please. I want to know everything, so don't leave anything out."

Rick looked pained.

Anne understood, "No really, Rick. I have only been guessing all of it up until now, and my guesses cannot be any more hurtful than what you might say. No matter what it is, I want to know it all. You can't hurt me with the explanation. It will only help. I promise."

"You are sure?"

She leaned over and kissed his cheek and then gently turned his face toward hers to look him in the eye. "Yes, I'm sure."

He touched his forehead to hers, "Okay, here goes."

He began by explaining that his sister had only known that he had been serious with a girl in college but nothing had happened with it. She knew no details about Anne. She had called him when she purchased her new house from the Elliotts.

"When she told me the house was in Eden Grove, I almost had a heart attack. I asked her what street it was on, never expecting that it would be your street," He looked at Anne, "I remembered your address because it was so ridiculous."

"You would make fun of me about it all the time." Anne laughed. "And it *is* ridiculous."

"So, when she said it was on Paradise Lane and after I teased her mercilessly, I asked her who the seller was, and she told me it was a family named Elliott. I couldn't believe it."

Rick went on to say how sick he felt for days because all of the pain and hurt from Anne's rejection came rushing back.

"In the end, after I calmed down, I couldn't wait to come see the house. I had to see where you had lived… to see if it smelled like you, and if I could feel you in the house. I was obsessed. I missed you so much."

Anne was surprised.

"Sophia invited me to come see it before they moved in, so the house was vacant. When I got there, I went from room to room to see if I could feel you or, I don't know…anything that would connect me with you again. There was only one room where I felt you. One of the bedrooms in the back of the house had a big window overlooking the backyard garden, and I envisioned you sitting in a chair looking out." He looked at Anne, "Was that your room? It was the one painted a really light blue"

Anne wiped a tear and nodded. "You could really feel me there?" He nodded and then looked upset that she was teary. She squeezed his hand and made him continue, "Keep going. Happy tears. I'm okay."

He explained that within a day or two, Sophia called him with news that she had met the Elliotts at the country club they had joined and was invited to dinner at one of their homes the next day.

"Hold on," Anne stopped him. "How did Sophia know about me?"

"What do you mean?"

"Well, when Dad and Elizabeth came home that night with the invitation to Mary's for dinner, they insisted that I was also invited because Sophia wanted to meet me. I couldn't figure out how your sister knew about me, and when I met her, she gave no indication that *you* had told her about me. I hadn't been at the club. In fact, I haven't been to the club in years. I doubt my membership is even current."

"Oh," Rick smiled and his eyebrow raised as he remembered, "This may surprise you. Sophia told me that while she was getting to know your sisters at the club, both of them could not stop talking about you. She had been asking questions about the house and both Mary and Elizabeth went on and on about your style and talents when it came to your old house. It was like they were in awe of you. That didn't jive with your description of how they treated you, so it made me curious. That was when I invited myself to come along."

"Wow, no way. I don't believe it." Anne shook her head. She couldn't wrap her head around what she was hearing about her sisters. It didn't make any sense. She was going to have to process this later.

Rick nodded and brought her hand up to his lips and kissed it, "I speak the truth."

They stared at each other for a minute until Jay interrupted,

"Okay, love birds…come on…get on with it."

Rick continued, "When I got to Mary's house, I don't know what I was expecting, but I had worked myself up into such a state of nervous anger that I couldn't think straight. I couldn't even look at you when you walked in the room on Charlie's arm, and as the evening wore on, I was so struck with how different you were, that I became even angrier."

"Different?" Anne was confused.

"You didn't speak. You didn't smile. You kept your eyes down," Rick looked pained again like it was hurting him to say all this. "You were acting like an abuse victim and I couldn't figure out why. I was going back and forth from being angry to feeling vilified. One moment I would be feeling a sort-of victory that you were unhappy without me, and then I would be overcome with sadness at your obvious unhappiness... but even with your altered behavior, it was hard not to stare at you the whole time. You were—*are*—as beautiful as I remembered."

"I had just been lectured by Elizabeth and Dad about my choice of outfit for the dinner...and I was unprepared for *you* being there. When I heard your voice at the front door, all I wanted to do was run home." Anne looked embarrassed. "Charlie found me in the powder room and gave me courage."

"I'm glad," Rick squeezed her hand, "I'll admit, though, that I was disappointed that you left after I came into the kitchen and finally spoke to you. I thought that meant that you were completely over me."

Rick then told them about being invited to the lake house, and that he was determined to go so that he could see more of Anne and figure out why she was so altered.

But when he got to the lake house, he was practically accosted by Lila. She had been relentless and wouldn't let him out of her sight.

"She wouldn't leave me alone. I have never been with a more determined flirt."

"You bet your life," Anne agreed. "Don't mess with a former cheerleader. That girl has always been a go-getter."

"Well, I felt go-getted constantly. Smothered is a better word."

"Just so you know," Anne added, "I had no idea you would be at the lake house. Elizabeth woke me up that morning and gave me 30 minutes to pack. I didn't find out you were there until June told me when I arrived. When Sophia came to find you in your room that first day and you spoke with her and Eliza in the hallway, I was sitting on the floor in my room up against the door with my head in my hands as I listened to your conversation. At that point I was resolved to stay in my room by myself for the whole two weeks so I could avoid having to be around you."

"Why?" Rick looked hurt.

"Because I was still in love with you and you had seemed indifferent towards me the night before. I wasn't sure I had the strength to deal with being ignored by you for that long."

"I think we were both experiencing a crazy mixture of emotions," Rick ran his fingers through his hair, "Did it ever occur to you that I was there just to be around you?"

"Nope," Anne shook her head, "If you had been friendly to me…if you had spoken to me…if you had even smiled, I probably would have been more comfortable. But you didn't do any of those things."

Rick looked so sad and sorry, "How can I ever apologize enough for my behavior for those two and a half weeks."

"You already have, and I have forgiven you, but I still need to know what was going through your head." Anne smiled, "And, thank you for saving me from falling when I was getting off the boat."

"What??" Sarah sat forward, "What happened on the boat?"

Anne told the story of Rick catching her so she wouldn't fall backwards with Wally in her arms.

"When I caught you, I could smell your hair, I didn't want to let go, but I felt like everyone was watching me…especially Lila…so I had to let you go before I wanted to."

"Yes," Anne agreed, "that was a nice moment, but you still didn't say anything, or smile, or give me any indication that you had forgiven me."

He started to say something, but Anne put her finger to his lips, "No more apologies. Just keep talking."

"I will admit that I was still a little mad, but just seeing you and being around you was making all those feelings melt away. I could see that you weren't happy either, and you weren't with someone else. I started to think that I may still have a chance with you, but then Lila wouldn't let me out of her sight. She kept me away from you. But, because I couldn't get near you, I was able to observe you. You are the most unselfish person I know. You took care of your nephews like you were their mother. I watched them spend more time with you than with Mary. You went to the hospital with Wally when he broke his arm instead of his own mom, because she wouldn't have been able to deal with it. I know how much you feared hospitals. You told me once that you were afraid to be a nurse because of that. Is that why you aren't a nurse?"

Anne nodded, "Partly. When I graduated, I was still mourning my mom, and hospitals scared me. I retreated into myself. I spent all my time at home alone, doing all the things for my family that my mom had done. I was afraid of everything."

"But not anymore," Sarah winked at Anne.

Rick looked back and forth between the girls. "What? …What am I missing?"

Anne explained, "I had decided when we moved that I was going to take the nursing boards and become a nurse. I needed to get out from under the oppression in my house. I had finally had it. I packed that entire house by myself…not one of my sisters helped me, or my dad. It is a bad habit on both sides that they expect me to do everything, and I go along with it. My dad and my sisters don't talk to me. It's not a great place to be if you are me. They resent me because I am like my mom, so they either criticize me or ignore me."

Rick squeezed her hand again, "I'm glad you have come to that realization. Now you just have to get out of that house."

"I already did," she smiled proudly. "I moved in with Jane when I left the beach house after Lila's accident. And I took the nursing boards two weeks ago."

"I'm so proud of you," Rick let go of her hand and put his arm around her and hugged her. He kept his arm around her, "Wait…Jane? Isn't she the one…?"

"Yes. She is the one who persuaded me that we

shouldn't get married when you asked me."

He frowned.

"Don't judge. She has been my most loyal advocate and support for these last 10 years. She gave me the courage and conviction to finally move out. She was my mom's best friend, and has been like a mom to me...the only person I could really talk to this whole time."

"Then I'm going to need to meet her and give her a piece of my mind, and then a big hug."

"And she will throw that piece right back at you and tell you that you were a fool for not listening to me in the first place."

Rick hung his head but grinned. "Agreed."

"So now tell me how I came to be invited here to the beach house?" Anne demanded.

"Well, I invited him and whoever he wanted to bring with him." Jay said like it was a secret.

Anne laughed, "Yes, I know that much. I want to know how he was able to get my name on the guest list."

They all looked at Rick to reveal this tidbit.

"Actually, when I got the message from Jay at the restaurant that night, I wracked my brain trying to figure out a strategy to get you in on the adventure without making it obvious, but I didn't have time to think it through because Lila had been looking over my shoulder at my phone and her eagle eyes read the text almost before I did. She started bouncing up and down in her seat and her father had to know what was going on. So...she blurted it out before I had a chance. Honestly, I had been trying to be polite with her for that entire two-week period, but this was the final straw for me. I was one deep breath away from denying there was even an invitation, and having a private chat with her after we got back to the house, when Landry declared that his girls could only go if Anne went, too."

"So, you went along because you wanted me to come to the beach house?"

"Yes, my dear. I knew you would love to see Sarah again, and I could get you away from your family. By then, I could tell that they were the reason for your altered behavior."

"I had my fingers crossed that you would consent to come with us," Rick added, "And at first you looked as if you would refuse, and then suddenly changed your mind."

"The only reason I agreed to go was because I could tell that Elizabeth was upset that she wasn't included." Anne admitted, "And I am ashamed to say that."

Rick continued, "The entire car ride to Malibu was spent trying to figure out how I was going to extricate myself from Lila's grasp and endear myself again to you." He paused, "Then we met Will and Luke, and I could tell that Will was interested in you. He never left your side from the moment we arrived."

"I know. Annoying." Anne laughed. "A little attention from the opposite sex was a nice change for me and I was initially flattered because, let's face it, he was hot." She winked at Rick, "but he was not my type, and I am sad that you really thought I would be interested in him."

"Yeah, well…" Rick had no more to say.

Sarah lightened the mood, "So what was it like being a cheerleader for a day and a half?"

"Oh my gosh!" Rick covered his face with his free hand, "Was she making the rest of you as crazy as me?"

Jay and Anne nodded. Sarah hadn't been there, so she could only imagine.

"I kept telling her to stop, but she wouldn't listen. I even told her that I may not be able to catch her every time. I didn't know that would be an almost fatal prediction."

"How long were you planning on continuing with her before you told her you weren't interested?" Anne was curious. "I mean, if she hadn't fallen."

"Well, that is the weird part." Rick looked concerned. "I had already told her I wasn't interested in her."

"What?" they all said at once and then mouthed, "jinx," to each other with pointed fingers.

"When?" Anne asked.

"The night before the hike when we were coming back from dinner on the pier, Chas and Henzie left us in the car to go for a walk and I took that private opportunity to tell her. She was okay with it. She even told me that even though I was 'hot' and everything; I was way too old for her."

"But she was hanging all over you on the hike," Jay added with raised eyebrows, "What was that all about?"

"I couldn't figure her out to save my life," Rick threw up his hands. "I just couldn't tell you. I had no clue."

He turned to Anne, "You don't know how much I wanted to be hiking with you. I wanted to insert myself in between you and Will so badly. I could hear you three laughing and I wanted to be a part of that. I wanted to get you away from him. You know, when you hugged me after I spoke to June, I almost bared my soul to you right then, but I could hear June still on the phone wanting to talk to you and then I heard the ambulance, so I pulled away."

Anne's eyes were wide, "I didn't want that hug to stop. And then you picked me up and carried me to the ambulance. I saw something in your eyes when you were carrying me that reminded me of the Rick I fell in love with. I hadn't felt that, yet."

"You messed with my hair and smiled at me. When you did that, I let myself believe that you might still have feelings for me."

"And then when you brought my change of clothes to the hospital? Why didn't you say anything then? You had to notice that I kept your sweatshirt on instead of the one you brought me."

"Did you notice that I brought the shirt you wore to Mary's for that first dinner?"

"Yes," Anne blushed, "You had to go through my things, which made me nervous."

Rick then answered her first question, "I didn't say anything at the hospital, even though I took the fact that you were still wearing my sweatshirt as a good sign, because you sat next to Will instead of me. And even though I knew that if you went from sitting by him, to sitting by me it would have looked odd to everyone in the room, it made me think twice that you two were together…and then he kissed you when he carried you into the house."

"WILL KISSED YOU?" Jay yelled and sat up. "What an idiot."

Anne laughed out loud, "Well, I was sound asleep, so I had no idea. I have only Rick's word that he did."

"That takes the cake right there." Jay's facial expression made everyone laugh.

"That is when I decided to leave." Rick admitted. "And if I had known that Will left before I did, I wouldn't have left. I just wish someone had told me."

"We found his note just before you left, but had no idea it would have made a difference." Sarah confirmed.

"And we didn't know why you left," Jay added, "you dumb-dumb."

Sarah stood up, grabbed Jay's hand to pull him up, and said, "Well, children, it's late and if we want to be able to find a parking place at the boardwalk tomorrow, we will need to leave here no later than nine. So, I, for one, need my beauty sleep. Good night to you both. It has been a really good day."

Jay agreed and as they left the room called out, "Love you both."

Anne leaned back against Rick and rested her head on his shoulder and they snuggled there for a few minutes until Rick stirred and echoed what Sarah had said about beauty sleep and all.

Anne was surprised, but was suddenly tired herself, and although she could have fallen asleep right there on the couch in Rick's arms, she recognized that she wanted to be rested for the festivities tomorrow.

Rick walked her to her room and they shared a long and tender kiss before he turned and walked to the stairs, where he blew her another kiss and mouthed, "I love you."

She fell asleep after thinking about the last few hours and re-reading his wonderful text message over and over.

Chapter 44

"Should I go wake him up?" Jay looked at the girls across the island countertop.

They had already eaten breakfast and were ready to go to the boardwalk, and had been waiting in the kitchen for Rick to make an appearance.

"Maybe?" Sarah nodded to Jay. But before Jay got halfway across the room, Rick came around the corner.

When he saw them all waiting and ready, he said, "I'm so sorry. I slept through my alarm." He went immediately to Anne, put his arm around her and gave her a kiss. "I didn't have the best night's sleep." He winked at Anne, "too many thoughts in my head."

Anne looked concerned because he looked exhausted, but he assured her he was fine and excited for the day's festivities.

They all piled into Jay's car and drove down to the pier.

There were people everywhere but they were able to find a place to park not too far from the boardwalk. Anne was in heaven just walking hand in hand with Rick. It didn't matter to her where they were…even standing in line at the DMV would have been lovely if Rick was there holding her hand. She couldn't believe all the feelings of hope and love and peace that she was feeling all at once.

"You haven't stopped smiling all morning," Sarah observed when they were looking in a booth with handcrafted jewelry. The boys were not interested in bracelets and had gone off to find something to drink.

"I know, right?" Anne blushed, "My face is starting to get sore. I need to frown for a minute." and she used both hands to massage her cheeks. "I just never thought I would ever be this happy."

"I'm sure it is a huge relief," Sarah gave Anne a side hug and then added, "What did you think of what Rick said about your sisters?"

"I'm not sure," Anne rolled her eyes, "Could they actually be that twisted to admire me that much and then treat me so horribly?"

"I don't know them, so I have nothing to offer."

"…Unless they were just bragging about a family member to a new friend just to show themselves off more."

"Anything is possible."

"Knowing them, I would tend to believe that they were just showing off, but then…" She paused thoughtfully, "I am just as much to blame, if I really think about it. I made the choice to let them walk all over me and treat me like they do. At first, I was just blindly doing what my mom would have done. I missed her so much. Maybe I was just trying to keep her close by doing all those things that she did. She was so good at taking care of everyone."

They both continued to walk among the vendors on the boardwalk for a few minutes.

"You know what?" Anne suddenly stopped. "I am going to get them each something: a peace offering of sorts. The way I am feeling right now…this happiness…has brightened my vision a little and I think that my unhappiness for the last 10 years has clouded my perception. All three of us are still stuck in a, sort-of, mourning for our mom. We have never talked about it. Never. I just realized that." Anne smiled to herself as if she had just solved a difficult puzzle.

"Well then, we have a mission," Sarah linked arms with Anne, "We are on a search for the perfect peace offering."

They walked from vendor to vendor searching for a gift for Mary and Elizabeth. They finally settled on tiny silver chain bracelets that had a little silver and gold daisy charm. Anne remembered that her mom's favorite flowers were daisies. She purchased one for her and her two sisters.

"Maybe I can start a conversation when I give them these," Anne mused, "Maybe we can start to heal and be sisters again."

She was resolved to somehow repair her relationship with her sisters. They needed each other. If Eliza and Mary weren't willing, then at least she could say she tried.

It was starting to get dark and the guys had not

returned. Sarah texted Jay to see where they were, and then made the comment: "They aren't shoppers. They are probably sitting on a bench somewhere eating an ice-cream."

"They better not be eating ice-cream!" Anne exclaimed. "Not without me, anyway."

Sarah's phone buzzed and Jay's message directed them to the far end of the boardwalk where they were sitting at tables by a food truck that was tempting them with gourmet mac and cheese. The girls walked quickly and found the boys drooling in the line for the mac and cheese, unable to decide which dish to order. In the end they each chose a different type of mac and cheese so they could all share, because they all wanted to try more than one. There was a shrimp one, a chicken one, one with tomatoes and onions, and one with zucchini and yellow squash. The tomato and onion one turned out to be the favorite, but not one morsel was wasted.

"Best food truck *ever*," Rick wiped his face with a napkin and then stood up, "Come on, it's getting darker and we should get a little closer to the pier before they start the fireworks."

They all made their way onto the sand where people had laid out blankets and set up chairs. Jay found a place up against some rocks next to the boardwalk where they could half sit on the rocks and watch the firework show.

Rick leaned against one of the rocks and pulled Anne in front of him into a close embrace and she leaned up against him with his arms wrapped around her. This would go down as the best 4th of

July in Anne's memory. Just being this close to him while the fireworks lit up the sky was the most romantic thing she had ever experienced. She could feel his breath on her ear and he would turn and lightly kiss her cheek every so often.

About five minutes into the fireworks, Rick got fidgety and suddenly stood upright and gently turned her around to face him. She looked into his eyes, which would light up with each light explosion. He took her hands in his and looked into her eyes so intently… with such a serious expression of love…It was so intimate that she almost started to cry.

Then he did something she didn't expect.

He dropped to one knee never taking his eyes off of her and let go of her hands. She felt her heart jump, and instinctively brought her hands up to cover her mouth. He reached out with his right hand and took her left hand and brought it to touch his lips as he gazed into her eyes, "Anne. My beautiful Anne." Then he lifted his left hand up to show her that the tip of his pinky finger held a ring. It was her ring. He had kept it all this time.

She started nodding furiously before he even got the words out.

"Wait, love," He chided with a grin, "I haven't said anything yet."

"Stand up so I can hear you over the fireworks," She leaned down and grabbed at his shirt to pull him up toward her. "I want to hear every word."

He stood up and lowered his head so he could be right near her ear. Chills ran up and down her spine.

"I have loved you for more than 10 years. I have

loved no other but you. Will you finally marry me?"

She pulled back a little so she could look in his eyes and then reached up with both hands to cradle his face. She closed the gap so that their lips were almost touching. Holding him there, she let her heart skip, and during that purposeful hesitation, he breathed out tenderly, "please."

It was then that she spoke just as tenderly, "Yes. A thousand times, yes," and then their lips barely touched. She could feel his breath intake sharply and then she allowed him to really kiss her. His lips were soft and slightly parted so she could feel him breathing. She didn't remember his kisses being like this. The butterflies in her stomach were keeping her from taking a full breath and she was getting dizzy. Her legs were getting shaky, too, but there was no way she was going to stop this. She was in heaven.

When their lips finally parted, she grabbed onto his shoulders to steady herself. Rick took a slight step back and took her left hand and slipped the ring on her finger. Anne looked at the ring on her finger for a moment as the lights flashed behind her and looked up at him with a smile that was so big it hurt her cheeks. Then she threw her arms around his neck and he lifted her up and kissed her again.

When Rick began turning around in a circle, the obvious movement next to them alerted Sarah and Jay, who had been cuddled up and engrossed in the fireworks display. When they looked over, at that very moment an unusually bright light flashed and they both saw the ring on Anne's finger as Rick spun her around.

Sarah squealed and spun around to give Jay a high-five and then a kiss.

As the finale of the fireworks erupted in nonstop explosions and bathed them in light, both couples turned their attention to the beauty before them, and kept their close embraces until the last of the lights died out.

Everyone else on the beach clapped and whistled and started gathering their blankets and moving toward their cars. Rick, Anne, Sarah, and Jay stayed right where they were until the boardwalk lights came back on so they could see each other more clearly.

There were hugs all around and congratulations offered, and then Anne said suddenly, "Wait a minute…where did the ring come from?"

Sarah jumped in too, "Oh my gosh, that's right! Do you *carry it with you*? You had no idea Anne was coming this weekend."

Rick held up his hand and grinned, "After you all went to bed last night, I drove home to get it." He yawned, "This is why I'm… sooo sleeeepy."

Anne punched him in the arm. "You nut!"

"That is over an hour each way," Jay was impressed.

Rick laughed, "I couldn't pass up this awesome proposal setting," and he opened his arms wide to indicate where they were standing. "That would have been lame."

Anne melted into his open arms and held on tight.

He wrapped his arms around her and swore he would never let go.

Influenced

.

Epilogue

Anne sat in her old room looking out the window at her mom's backyard garden. The spring flowers had just begun blooming so it was sea of color. The orange and lemon trees were also blooming, so the scent wafting in from her open window was divine.

There was a knock at her door, and then Sarah walked in with a garment bag.

"Let's get this party started," Sarah winked and hooked the bag onto the doorframe of the bathroom. She unzipped the bag to reveal Anne's wedding dress. Sarah was wearing a light blue, empire waist dress in flowy chiffon with cap sleeves. Anne had chosen the empire waist style because Sarah's little baby bump was starting to show.

"You look beautiful," Anne jumped up and threw her arms around her friend.

"Thank you, but we need make sure you look better than me."

Anne laughed, "Mary did my make up, and

Elizabeth did my hair," She backed up and let Sarah see her, "What do you think?"

"So, things are good between you guys?" Sarah asked as she looked over Anne's hair and makeup. She was still a little worried about the sister issues. She didn't want anything to ruin Anne's day.

"We still have moments, but for the most part, after I gave them the bracelets and made them sit and talk about Mom, things have been way better. I don't let them make assumptions anymore. They were more excited to be a part of the wedding than I thought they would be."

Sarah gave Anne's hair and makeup a thumbs-up. "You look like a hot model. Absolutely gorgeous! Rick is going to pass out."

Elizabeth had swept Anne's auburn hair into a loose bun with different braids wrapped around, and with loose curly tendrils that hung around her face. She really did look like a model, but then Sarah had always considered her friend beautiful even though Anne would never have agreed.

As Sarah helped Anne into her dress, Anne told her about her new job at the children's hospital. She had decided to be a neo-natal nurse, and she was already a favorite among the doctors and new parents.

Anne's dress was also an empire waist dress, but the bodice had three quarter sleeves, and a square cut neckline. The fabric was a rose-patterned, satin brocade. The rest of the dress was simple straight chiffon in the front, and a mass of large pleats of chiffon in the back.

As they both looked at Anne in the big mirror,

Anne got emotional, "I wish my mom could see me."

"Now, stop that, you can't ruin your make up," Sarah tried to lighten Anne's spirits to quell the tears, "Tell me again how we are standing in your old room."

"Well, when we were here for Thanksgiving, Sophia asked about where we were thinking of having the wedding, and Rick and I hadn't really even picked a date yet." Anne said, "Jane had offered her backyard, you offered the Malibu house, and I told her all of that. Then she got all serious on us and asked me what my dream wedding had looked like when I was younger. I hadn't wanted to say anything, or assume anything, but I told her that my mom had landscaped our backyard—this backyard—with the intention of having all three of her daughters use it for their weddings. After she died, Mary decided that she wanted her wedding to be at the club, and then we had to move, so I had given up on my mom's plan."

Anne's eyes filled up with tears, "Sophia told me that there was no reason not to fulfill my mom's dream. So, we set a date right then. It was perfect."

Sarah got a tissue and Anne blotted her tears without messing up her make-up. Mary had said she could cry all she wanted and none of it would come off, and she was right.

"It's time." Sarah smiled at Anne and they embraced once more before leaving the room and heading downstairs.

Walt was waiting at the bottom of the stairs and gave Anne a kiss and a hug. "I love you Anna-bella.

You look radiant."

"Thank you, Dad." Anne took his arm, kissed his cheek, and they walked to the side door.

Elizabeth and Mary stood by the door waiting in their blue chiffon dresses and each held one yellow gerbera daisy. Sarah was holding one white gerbera daisy and Anne's bouquet, which was a fist full of yellow and white gerbera daisies tied with a thick white French ribbon. They were all smiles. The sisters had decided that they would all wear their daisy bracelets to honor their mother.

Mary opened the door and stepped around the corner to signal the musicians that they were ready, and the processional music began playing.

Mary gestured to Wally, who had been sitting on a kitchen chair swinging his legs, and he blew Anne a kiss and walked out the door to go down the aisle first with the ring pillow. Then Elizabeth followed him, and then Mary. Sarah winked at Anne when it was her turn, and whispered, "Your groom looks *hot*!" and then disappeared out the door.

Anne got goosebumps and suddenly couldn't wait to see Rick. Her heart was pounding as she realized that she had waited almost 11 years for this day. She held on to her dad and they started out the door.

As they turned the corner and started down the aisle, she could see Rick standing under the arbor waiting for her in his black tux. Sarah was right. He was *hot*. She wanted to run to him, but contained herself and stayed in a slow step with her dad. As she got closer, she could tell that he was emotional. He reached up to wipe his eyes at least twice, but he never took his eyes off of her. He was grinning ear to ear. He looked so handsome standing there smiling at her. Her heart skipped a beat each time she thought about being with him forever.

By the time she and her dad got all the way up the aisle, she had tears in her eyes, and when her dad gave her one last kiss on her cheek, he handed her a tissue, and placed her hand into Rick's.

She held onto Rick's hands during the ceremony and looked up into his eyes, and hoped that he could feel the love that she was feeling for him. His eyes were filled with love for her.

It was hard to concentrate, but she tried hard to hear and internalize everything that was said. When she heard, "you may kiss your bride," and Rick leaned in to kiss her, she closed her eyes and let his lips find hers. They were both trembling with nerves and excitement. Then she reached her arms around his neck and he picked her up in the middle of the kiss as everyone applauded and shouted.

"You are so hot!" She whispered into his ear, and he chuckled.

"And you are the most beautiful woman I have ever seen."

As he kissed her again, she heard the words she'd been waiting 11 years to hear.

"Ladies and Gentlemen, it is my pleasure to introduce, Mr. and Mrs. Frederick Wentworth II."

ABOUT THE AUTHOR

Jennifer Goodman raised four children, and is a grandmother of one (so far). She teaches middle school language arts at a private school in Southern California. She enjoys jigsaw puzzles, watching Dodger games, and doing 16-square sudoku.

Check out another title by Jennifer Goodman:

Single No More

Andrew has fallen for James' sister, Claire, but they have never met. He just feels a strong connection to her photograph and wants to see if the connection is real. James has made several attempts to set them up, but Claire refuses. She was treated badly in a past relationship and has sworn off love for herself, but is, ironically, a successful director of a popular dating show on television. James comes up with a plan to have Andrew apply to be on the dating show so he can meet Claire. Andrew is willing but hesitant. Will James' plan backfire? Or will Andrew and Claire find a connection that motivates her to break down the walls that she has built around her heart?

Made in the USA
Las Vegas, NV
14 July 2024

92319452R00144